Sands of Time

by

Bruce A. Sarte

Credits
Cover Artist: Bruce A. Sarte
Editor: Carady Madden

ISBN: 9780982981634

Bucks County Publishing
202 North 7th Street
Bally, PA 19503

Dedication

I would like to dedicate this book to my wife, Erin.
Without whom I would have never been able to finish the story.

Acknowledgements

I would like to thank my wife Erin for her encouragement and support while I sat in bed whining that I couldn't concentrate. I would also like to thank two of the most influential literary influences in my life, Jeff Cain and Verne Romefelt. Mr. Cain taught me how to think about what I was writing and Commander Romefelt taught me how to write what I was thinking.

March 1st

In the blink of an eye, the sound gripped my heart and tore the soul from my still and helpless body.

I heard the screech of tires preceding the violent collision of two polar opposite forces, right before the wretched smell of burning rubber reached me, and then there was nothing. Silence.

It's always the silence that gets me, every time I hear it… and I hear it all the time… all day… all night.

The deafening silence that only solitude, loneliness, and guilt can bring.

As soon as I heard the silence, I knew what it was. The sound of the car going into the water; the sound of my wife trying desperately to get out; the sound of my children screaming for someone… maybe even me. What is the sound of a life ending? What about the sound of my life ending? It didn't matter if I ran or walked… but I ran. I didn't have to see the skid marks to know what happened… but I saw them anyway.

It happened so fast. I watched in disbelief as my entire world exploded in a ball of fire and pain.

As I sit and watch the sun set on yet another day of solitude, I realize it is just another ball of fire that burns a hole in my soul every day, a hole that will never heal. And just like a cancer that spreads uncontrollably through the dying body, this pain infects every inch of my being. And I treat it as any good doctor would... when there is no cure, but you can numb the pain and make it bearable, that is what you do. That's where the drinking comes in.

Was today any better than yesterday... or the day before... or the day before that? Are things getting better? The holidays came and went, and I barely even noticed. I could say that the holidays were terrible and that I missed

Sandy and the kids more then I ever thought I could miss anyone or anything.

Yes, I could say that, because I am sure it would be the truth if I had even the slightest recollection of Christmas or New Year's. I can only assume that there was a Christmas because it happens every year, with or without me. But the truth is I was so mind-numbingly drunk that I can't remember a moment of it, and

I don't even care.

I could say that I drown myself in my work. During the off-season, our little pub does a thrifty business selling alcohol and food. I could say that, but it's not true. I've barely paid any attention to the pub or the inn. It has been six months since Sandy and the kids were taken from me, and in that time, I have downed more bottles of Jack than all of my customers combined have bought and consumed in the last two years. So, it stands to reason that the inner numbness afforded to me by the warm, personal relationship with my new best friend, Mr. Daniels, has not allowed me to feel the pain… or should I say, has allowed me to skip the whole hurting part of this process.

My shrink says that I need to grieve and accept the loss and move on.

Why? What kind of an evil, sadistic bastard is this doctor? Why would anyone subject himself to the cavernous abyss that is inside of me? Dr. Ashton says that if I look inside myself, I'll find some sort of inner peace or something stupid like that. Why would I look inside myself when looking inside a bottle allows me to drown myself in the acceptance that only Mr. Daniels can offer?

Dr. Ashton wants to see me weekly; he says I need help to accept what happened. I say acceptance is for pansies and I've already got help, so screw that. Dr. Daniels — hey, Jack would like that; he's a doctor now — Dr. Daniels is working wonders on my coping skills. Nothing bothers me now. What does that quack Ashton know that Dr. D can't offer me? I won't be seeing Ashton anytime soon.

Healing? Who needs to heal when you can be numb?

What I *do* remember from the holidays is mostly sitting in my office with

Jack. Just sitting there, listening to music and singing along to whatever happened to come on, even if I didn't know the words. Well, if you could call that delirious drivel that was coming out of my mouth singing — but only Jack was judging me, and he tends to be very kind. Especially after a few glasses from his glimmering walls of acceptance.

I did have the inn to run, but in the winter, we are rarely busy. Not too many people vacationing at the Jersey Shore over the holidays and cold weekends. They tend to make their way to the warmer climates or the ski slopes for vacation in the winter months. Oh, we do get a guest here and there, just looking to get away and spend a weekend overlooking the scenic Atlantic, even though it is cold. Some people like that, watching the waves coming in and out even though they know the water is frigid—they tell me they find it comforting. It just makes me want to walk into the cool, flowing waves of the ocean. Step by step, I can feel the water on my feet, grabbing at my ankles, pulling me in. Step by step, my knees are wet in the clutches of the dark and dreary ocean. It pulls me… beckons me further into its cold and welcoming arms. There is no instinct to retreat, no need to turn around, just the welcoming cold of the icy grip of the ocean on my waist beckoning me to continue… step by step… and I just keep going until the undertow grabs me and pulls me under.

So, needless to say, running the inn in the winter is nary a concern. Besides, Natalie pretty much runs the place for me. She's smart, confident, and understands how I like things… which is very important to me. When I first hired her, I wanted someone who would run the inn the way I would. She's that person. I'd be lost without her; the inn would be lost without her. There was a time when we had a nice relationship… it was fun… we'd crack little jokes, and she would keep me up to date on what was going on when I was busy with other things…

But since Sandy and the kids were taken from me, I have fallen into this distant, disinterested, hollow numbness that is my current personality, and she began to respond likewise. She acts more concerned and watchful than before… we don't have that easy conversation anymore… no more jokes, no more laughter. Even with the great responsibility that being my front desk manager carries with it, we never really had an employee–employer relationship.

We were more like good friends who worked together. And now, it seems like that cold workplace interaction that you see in TV. I would say it's very sad, but I'm not sure I remember what it is to be sad. How does it feel? How does anything feel? I've forgotten. I've forgotten a lot of things.

How to feel is just one of them...

Dr. Ashton has convinced me that writing is cathartic... Is it?

I guess we'll find out.

March 4ᵗʰ

The guests come and go and I hardly notice anymore. I used to love this.

The hustle and the bustle of the inn... but now the inn runs itself for the most part. I haven't really been making the day-to-day decisions. I have left much of it to my staff to take care of, and they've been very good about it. Thank God for Natalie. She's been invaluable the past few months. She's young and sweet, and she works very hard. She treats this inn as if it were her own. Maybe she deserves a raise? I'll have to remember to see if I can swing that for her... or maybe just a nice big Christmas bonus this year. God knows that didn't even occur to me this past year. I wonder if everyone hates me for that?

The rest of the staff doesn't really speak to me very much anymore.

Actually, they seem to go out of their way to avoid me, all except Curtis, my head bartender. He listens... offers some advice and a straight-faced joke or two to keep my spirits up. We've been friends ever since we met in high school, and our friendship has withstood many of life's ups and downs.

After high school, our paths went in very different ways for many years. I went off to college, and he hopped in his Mustang convertible and took a long road trip. He drove around the country, working odd jobs to pay for gas and food. It was quite the experience—he saw the country and learned how to make something out of nothing. I, on the other hand, went to college. I learned how to drink my body weight in beer, pick up girls, sleep with them, leave in the middle of the night, get two hours sleep and still get up in the morning. Add to that the bonus skill of pretending I was interested in what the stuffed shirt at the head of the room was talking about. Who made out better? Hard to say, really, but you could easily argue that his path was the wiser one. Either way, he runs the pub and does a hell of a job—it always makes a profit. Even with my pilfering of the Jack.

The others… they ask how I'm doing, if they can do anything… it's all just niceties, really. They don't really care, so I tell them I'm fine and no, I'm getting through it, thanks… I mean, what would they do if I told them the truth?

"I'm dying inside! I have nothing left! I would not care either way if a demon from hell grew inside of me and devoured my soul, leaving nothing but the empty shell of a broken and hollow man. That is what I am anyway, so what would it really matter? I am NOT OKAY! Nothing is okay, nobody cares, and no one is even capable of understanding, so stop asking! My heart has been ripped from my chest, has dried up and turned to stone right in front of my eyes— do you have the elixir for the virus that has broken my soul into as many pieces as the sky has stars? Does the sky still have stars? I haven't noticed…"

If given the chance, I think most of my employees would run as far away from me as possible.

Tonight the door to my study slowly opened, and one my bartenders told me we're out of gin. I picked up the phone and started dialing my alcohol distributor. It rang a few times before I realized how late it was, and that the sales guy wasn't going to be there. I told the bartender I'd have to call in the morning, and he shuffled out and closed the door.

I don't even remember his name. I know he has worked here for four years, but still I cannot remember his name. It seems I'm pretty good at remembering the girls' names... but not the guys'. How pathetic is that?

And I've only had three glasses of Jack. I'm surprised we're not out of

Jack. Surprised, but thankful—hey, at least I have something to be thankful for.

Everything's coming up roses... Maybe I'll throw a party.

I went there last night; to the one place I haven't been... to the one place that can make me feel—to the church. After the guests were settled and the lobby area was quiet, I grabbed my coat and my savior. I went out through the lobby and saw Natalie at the front desk. I told her I was going to the church for a while and would be back later. She looked at me like a sad puppy and told me to take as much time as I needed, that she was on until 6 anyway. That's my Natalie, always dependable and always helpful. I just wish she'd stop treating me like a shell-shocked war veteran. And in some ways, I'd almost prefer to have post-traumatic stress syndrome.

I could tell that she knew I had been drinking, and I wasn't doing a really good job of hiding Jack in my coat. She didn't say a word, but it was that look of genuine concern she gave me as I pushed through the door that stayed with me.

It was almost as if she was reaching out and begging me to let her help. But it was likely my fertile imagination or the seed that Jack planted in my mind. She's sweet, but why would she want to help me? Probably just worried the inn will run into the ground and she'll lose her job.

I saw her smile sweetly as the door closed and heard her gently remind me that she was here if I needed her. For what? To heal my wounds? To soothe my soul? Or for work? What could she do for me? She's sweet. Did I say that already? I guess Jack is still hanging around in my head. How many glasses have I had? I forget... counting becomes a challenge after a while. Outside it was dark and quiet and cold, but at the time, I didn't notice. I found Sandy's grave and sat down, leaning against the tombstone. The cold, hard granite... it's as comforting and welcoming as my bed has become since she's been out of my life...

SANDRA JEAN SHEPARD
BORN: MAY 15TH, 1974
DIED: SEPTEMBER 1ST, 2004
BELOVED MOTHER AND WIFE
OUR LIVES ARE EMPTY WITHOUT HER

Empty. Our lives... her grave. When you think about it, it all makes sense. They never found the bodies from the crash, and I still haven't found my soul. Everyone assumed they were burned beyond recovery in the fire or thrown from the car into the ocean and that their bodies never washed ashore. None of it made sense to anyone, least of all me. I am so tired trying to make sense of it all... of anything anymore.

Yes, anything... that's the right word. I leaned in, took a swig and started to cry. The tears came from me as if my eyes were melting, slow and warm.

Then they just began to flow more freely. I cried for what seemed like forever.

Then I got angry... again.

"WHY? Why did you have to do that? Why did you always run?! It was always about you and your precious comfort. You never stepped out of your little comfort zone, not for me, not for anyone. You didn't like something, it didn't happen. We always fought over it, and you always ran away. You'd run... like a child! WHY? You ran from everything! Including me, including our family... And now you've run out of my life and taken our children with you. You took the children; YOU TOOK TYLER AND CAITLYN, DAMN YOU! I hope you're happy because my life is worthless now... without you... without Tyler... without

Caitlyn..." I was crying openly now. "God damn you... I loved you so much, I still love you; why did you have to leave?"

Then I heard something... felt something. Like someone was there, or like

I was being watched. I jumped to my feet and immediately fell down to my knees... I was very dizzy. Quickly, I tried to recover and find out who was there.

But I couldn't see anyone. It was just me. I felt it, though. Maybe I should give Jack the rest of the night off.

I didn't go to Tyler and Caitlyn's graves... I couldn't. They were right there, but I couldn't look. Five feet away... Not even a glance... But I could feel them; I thought I could sense their presence, and I couldn't bear it, the weight of the lives not lived, the love never given, the smiles never seen… not even Jack could help me.

Then I heard the footsteps. Someone was here; someone was following me. I couldn't move, but I could hear them coming. Then I saw the flashlight. It was moving back and forth over the headstones two aisles away. Stop, start, swing left to right. I tried to get to my feet, tried to balance so I could hide, but I just fell over again. The flashlight came my way. I tried to lie as still as possible.

I even stopped breathing. Then I felt wetness on my arm. Jack was spilling out onto my coat, dammit. I reacted quickly to keep Jack from completely emptying out all over the ground and me. I needed him. Then the flashlight was on me.

"Sam? Is that you? Sam Shepard? It's Pastor Paul."

What was Pastor Paul doing out here at this time of night? What was I going to say to him? Was I going to stand here, staggering, and explain why I was here? And then add the gripping story of why I was drunk out of my mind?

Not likely. And then he was in front of me.

"Sam, my word! Are you okay? Here, let me help you up."

I was laying flat on my back, drunk, with an open, half-spilled bottle of

Jack Daniels in my hand and reeking of the alcohol. What must have been going through his mind? I could only imagine. But as I took his outstretched hand, all I could feel was concern. I looked into his eyes, and all I could see was empathy and worry. I was finally able to get to my feet and balance myself on some poor soul's headstone.

"Sam, are you alright? What is going on? I haven't seen you since…"

His voice trailed off, and he looked away. "Since Sandy and the kids."

I looked directly into his eyes, and I couldn't hide the pain.

"Sam, if you are here searching for something, searching for someone, for an answer… God has those answers."

"Pastor, I…" I stammered, but just couldn't get the words out. "I really don't think that I am the kind of person God wants around, and I don't think He has what I am looking for."

"God is always with you, always there, whether you can see it or not. The things you have been through are too painful to endure alone, without the comfort of the Lord."

I stood straight up, fire in my eyes and venom in my mouth.

"With all due respect, God has taken everything from me that means anything. He took away my racing, my wife, and my children. The only thing I have left is that inn, and when it comes right down to it, I just don't have the heart for it anymore."

My eyes burned through Pastor Paul. But all he did was put his hand on my shoulder. He looked at me with genuine concern.

"Sam, I know that you feel alone and that you think God has forsaken you.

He has not. I am not going to force you into anything, but when you're ready, He will lead you, and I will be here for you."

I couldn't respond; I could only stare, and I wanted to cry.

"Sam, don't think you have been forsaken. I have the feeling that God has blessed you more than you think." He was looking at me a little too carefully.

"Do you need help getting home?"

I looked away, then down at the bottle.

"I've got all the help I need." I glanced back at Pastor Paul, then pushed past him and walked into the night. I looked at the bottle as I stumbled away and decided Jack wasn't quite done for the night. I finished the bottle and continued to stumble home.

The inn was quiet when I finally fell into the lobby. I have no idea what time I finally dragged my sorry self onto the carpet and fell onto the couch in the middle of the lobby. I looked up to see Natalie's sexy little body behind the desk, where she was reading a book. She looked up as I noisily flopped onto the cushion.

"Sam, everything is quiet. Someone called down with a question about how late the boardwalk was open. I told them that everything closes pretty early in March, but that's all. That was around midnight, I guess—it's almost 4 am now." The she looked at me with concern. "Are you okay? Do you need help?"

I think I was actually drooling; I'm so disgusting. "No," I managed to slur.

How suave and debonair I was. But I think my inability to keep my head centered on my body gave her the impression that I was lying, so she came over to help anyway. I was a terrible liar, especially when I was this wasted. And I was seriously wasted. I had consumed more Jack then ever before.

"Sam, it's okay; I can help you... please let me help you." She put her arm around my waist, and I wrapped my

arm around her tiny shoulders as she helped me up. Her shoulders felt so nice.

"We're friends, Sam. I wish you would let me help you. Let me be there for you—I can listen."

But I'm not sure if she was actually talking to me. She could have simply been talking out of frustration. She helped me out to the carriage house I lived in just behind the inn, then guided me into my room and sat me on my bed. Wow, I thought, she is really beautiful. Her dark hair and warm chestnut eyes looked so understanding and comfortable and... forgiving. She was looking at me, our faces inches apart—that was because my arms were still around her shoulders.

"Sam, sit down and I'll help you into bed."

Help me into bed? Sounds like a plan to me. My arms slowly retreated from her soft and delicate shoulders. Her body was thin and fit—apparently, she exercised and took care of herself. Wow, she is beautiful; did I say that already?

I tend to repeat myself when Jack is around... My hands paused at the small of her back, but my drunken attempt to pull her toward me was clumsily thwarted by my lack of motor skills. My arms fell harmlessly away onto the bed. I looked up at her while she reached down to help me swing my legs up into bed. She didn't seem to notice that, as she pulled the covers back, her small yet firm breasts brushed my cheek. And I turned and kissed her left breast ever so lightly. She paused... slightly, just for a moment, and then continued. Not saying a word.

She was trying to help me get into bed slowly, but I really fell into bed at that point. She turned to leave.

"Nat?"

"Yes, Sam?"

"Stay here… with me… tonight, please?"

"Sam, you know I can't do that."

"Oh, no," I slurred, "don't worry; it won't be a problem, I promise. It won't be weird or anything… I just…"

"Sam, someone has to be at the front desk." She glanced back at me with a smile that was mixed worry with concern. "I have to go." And she quickly but quietly closed the door. I think I was asleep before the door latched shut. I'm such an ass sometimes.

Sometimes?

March 5th

I have no idea what Natalie thought. I don't know what I wanted her to think. I don't even know why I asked her to stay—other than I just didn't want to be alone. But I'm sure we both know what would have happened if she had stayed. I would have done more than just kiss her breast, and it would have ended badly. She's too smart and knows better than to put herself in a bad situation like that. You don't mix love and work, that's all. What if it's not love? No... that option seems bad, too.

And what did the pastor think? Right now, I don't give a damn what God thinks, but Pastor Paul has always been kind to the family and me. I should call and apologize... but then he would probably give me the whole "God" thing again, and I just can't listen to it.

I pulled myself up in the morning and snuck away into my office. Surfed

the Internet for most of the day. Checked eBay for WWII memorabilia, then read the news on CNN and downloaded Kenny Chesney's new album from iTunes. You'd think I would have listened to the new album, since I just paid $9.99 for it, but no. Instead, I listened to "I Go Back" over and over again... because I do; I go back every day... every day. To the argument... to her running out the door crying... telling myself that I wasn't running after her... not this time. Forget it.

But what if I had...just one more time?

My phone rang around 10:30, and I let it ring until it went to voicemail.

When I checked the message, it was Pastor Paul calling to see if I was okay. I really just can't talk to him right now, I told myself. I guess I just don't know why.

Is it because I don't want to hear about God? Or because I am too embarrassed? Or both? And maybe because I am afraid that he is telling me the truth.

My phone rang again around 11:00. I decided to answer this time, and it was Stephanie at the front desk. There was a problem with one of the guest's reservations. Why was she calling me? They all used to come right into my office, without even knocking. They are so put off by me it has come to this: A phone call. So I went to the bathroom, washed my face and straightened myself up, and went to see what was going on.

A young blonde lady was with Stephanie at the desk. Stephanie was one of our interns from Rutgers business school—she was good with the guests and did a good job overall.

"Hello, my name is Sam and I am the owner of the inn. How can I help?"

The fantastically beautiful blonde woman looked at me and smiled. Wow, nice smile. Her green eyes sparkled as she tried not to look annoyed, but I could see a tension there. I had to make an effort not to stare at those deep green eyes. They grabbed me and seemed to not let go. I was afraid of getting lost in them.

"It seems my reservation is not in the computer. I made it online a few days ago. I even have my e-mail confirmation with me," — she handed it to me —

"but the young lady here says I don't have a reservation. I... I don't know what to say, really, other than I made the reservation, it's paid for, and I need somewhere to stay." I read over her e-mail confirmation:

EMILY NOBLE
GUESTS: 1
DATES: MARCH 5 THROUGH MARCH 10
TYPE: JEFFERSON
STATUS: PAID
CONFIRMATION NUMBER: 12012004J

"Miss Noble, everything does seem to be in order." I stepped behind the counter and checked our reservation status for the weekend. "Let me just take a look at our computer."

I noticed that the Jefferson was indeed reserved, but it didn't have anyone's name or confirmation number on it. This happened sometimes with our Internet registration system. I glanced at Emily; she looked like she was going to fall over and I needed to find somewhere for her to land.

"Here we are." I handed her the keys to the Jefferson Suite, which was one of our finer suites in the inn. She must be a fairly well-to-do young lady to be staying here alone in that suite. No wedding ring, either. Is she someone's lover, perhaps, stashed away for a long weekend? No matter, not my business. But sometimes it pleasantly helped pass the time to wonder... and there was something about her. Something that made me want to know.

"I'll have one of our staff members help you with your bags, and I will send a complimentary Patriot Basket to your room to try and make up for the inconvenience."

She smiled. "No, really, it's not a problem. I just need my room, that's all."

"Not at all, and here is my card if you need anything while you are here, or even if you have questions or would like to make future reservations here at the Patriot Inn."

Or if you wanted to go out sometime and spend a romantic evening by the fire, or perhaps a naked evening in a hot tub… that would be okay, too. At that moment, she looked at me and smiled. Almost like she heard my thoughts and was agreeing to the sordid affair I was playing out in my head.

Emily started towards her room, and I trudged back to surf the Internet some more… maybe even order that gin we needed for the bar. I checked the stock of Jack Daniels while I was at it—better drunk then sorry.

Listened to "I Go Back" some more… Hey, this writing thing is helping.

Yeah, maybe if I keep telling myself that, I won't need Jack anymore. Oh, yeah, there he is… Come here, old buddy!

March 6th

Sandy and I purchased The Patriot Inn ten years ago, after my accident. I had been driving NASCAR for five years and had won quite a few races. I was a promising driver with my whole career in front of me. I was in second place in the points standing when I had the wreck that ended my career. It was a hot day in Indianapolis during the Brickyard 400. The heat had caused me to make a tire change earlier than I would have normally made one. I was running side by side with another car when my right front tire blew out. The investigation showed that the sidewall of the tire was faulty. It pulled me right into the wall, which spun me around and flipped the car. The car began to violently tumble end over end until it finally came to rest in the infield. I couldn't move or feel anything. I thought I was dead. Lucky me, I had only damaged several vertebrae and was paralyzed.

Through several operations, a lot of rehab, and the love of a good woman,

I regained my ability to walk and almost 100% of my physical capacity before the accident. Except for driving. I can't sit in a car for any length of time. My back begins to hurt, and I get sharp, excruciating pains shooting up my spine. The doctors say it's all in my head. So is everything else, right?

The inn is in Point Pleasant Beach, New Jersey, conveniently located about two hours from New York City and Philadelphia. That line is right out of the brochure on the front desk. The inn isn't on the beach—it's three blocks away from both the beach and the Manasquan inlet. But from our Jefferson and

Washington Suites, you can see the ocean and the inlet. Guests can walk to the beach, the inlet, or into town to do some antiquing or eat at one of the many restaurants. We get a lot of guests from the city that love the quiet, beach atmosphere of the inn but still want the proximity to New York, Philadelphia, and

Atlantic City. I used to love it, too. Sandy and I would daytrip out to Atlantic City and spend the day walking along the boardwalk, grab dinner, and head back home. Those days were some of the best days of my life. We loved those times.

I don't think I'll ever go there again. I miss her so much.

Tyler and Caitlyn used to like to go to Philadelphia. We'd go to the art museum and or a Phillies game. Caitlyn wasn't crazy about baseball and Tyler wasn't into art, but they would compromise and spend half the day doing one and half doing the other without much complaining. After the game, we'd all head over to South Street and get ice cream and coffee. The kids loved looking through the stores and taking carriage rides around Headhouse Square. We had so much fun; they were good kids and loved to laugh and experience what the city had to offer. I wish we could do that again... just one more time. I miss them... I miss them a lot…They were good kids; I just wish I had been a good dad. I need a drink.

I retired to my office for my nightly ritual of listening to music and drinking with Jack. I was queuing up what I called my "Misery Mix" in iTunes and getting out my favorite drinking glass when the phone rang.

"Hello, Sam Sheperd." "Wish You Were Here" by Pink Floyd started up.

"Mr. Sheperd, this is Emily Noble in the Jefferson Suite. I don't know if you remember me, but we met earlier." Remember? I was picturing her in a sexy black lace nightgown right now.

"Well, hello, Miss Noble. How can I help you this evening?" Perhaps your shirt is stuck on, and you need some help biting it off?

"I'm having some trouble with the lights in my room, and I didn't know who else to call. What can I do to get some help?"

"I'll be right up to take a look…. Ummm," I stumbled here, "Is it okay for me to come up now? I mean, are you, aaaa… Are you…?"

"Dressed?" She laughed, a light and comforting laugh. "Yes, I am. For now. I'd appreciate you coming up." Was that a little phone flirting I heard?

"Okay, I'll be right up, bye." I didn't even hear her say goodbye as my face flushed with embarrassment. Could I have sounded a little dumber?

I went up to the Jefferson Suite and knocked. Emily Noble opened the door, dressed in a stunning little black dress with black stockings on and no shoes. The outfit really enhanced her breasts and her backside very nicely, and I had a hard time not staring, especially as she looked at me. It was her eyes again—they penetrated me. Almost as if she knew every thought I was having, and her smile seemed to say, "I know I look fantastic in this dress. Go ahead, keep looking."

"What seems to be the trouble?"

"The light switch in the bathroom stopped working, and I wanted to take a nice hot bath in your lovely claw-foot tub, but I can't see anything."

I tried it to confirm… switch on, no lights. I checked the bulbs and they looked fine, so I opened up the wall plate and noticed that the wires were loose.

Odd, but it was quickly fixed, and click… lights on.

"Oh, wonderful!" She smiled, and I think she even bounced a little. I noticed on the sitting area table and that the Patriot Basket, which consisted of

Asher's Chocolates and a bottle of Chaddsford Winery Merlot, was untouched.

"Is the basket not to your liking, Miss Noble?"

"Oh, no, it's lovely. I just haven't had a chance…" She trailed off. "Just haven't been… in the mood, I guess." And her pretty face looked troubled for a moment, but as quickly as it came, the expression went away. Her lover not coming? Perhaps they broke it off. Business deal gone awry? There I go again… none of my business.

"And please, my name is Emily."

"Alright, Emily. I'll leave you to your bath. Is there anything else I can help you with tonight?" As quickly as it came out, I realized how it sounded. And the look on her face confirmed I'd misspoken. "I mean…"

Then she laughed. "I know what you meant, Mr. Shepard, and no, I'll be okay… at least for tonight." She smiled, and I walked to the door. As I closed it behind me, I said, "Please, it's Sam. Goodnight, Emily."

"Goodnight, Sam."

March 8th

There are just those days and times... moments... evenings... weeks... that you just want to have back. I wish I had that night with Sandy back... I could have made a difference. I could have stopped her, grabbed her and screamed,

"NO! DON'T GO! YOU WON'T COME BACK!" Sometimes when I think that, I wonder if she was even going to come back anyway.

But, yesterday was just one of those days. It started out well enough... I woke up and had a little energy — that is to say, I wasn't completely hung over. I went down to the lobby hoping to accidentally run into Emily, but she either wasn't up yet or was already out. It was a beautiful sunny Saturday, after all.

Most people would want to be outside and enjoying it. I made my way into the pub to make myself an omelet, some coffee, and a glass of orange juice. Emily probably polished off that bottle of wine in her hot, steamy bubble bath... and I missed it.

Natalie was working the day shift. She always works the day shift on

Saturdays so she can host her Bible study group on Saturday nights. From what she tells me, it sounds like a good time—they even mix up a pitcher of margaritas. A strange combination, the Bible and margaritas, but who am I to judge? And in true form, I seem to have forgotten about her raise already, damn.

Note to self: *Find money.*

Natalie and I had a brief conversation about a problem with the lighting outside. I have always wanted to rip it all out and upgrade the whole outside lighting system with a state-of-the-art system that I can control from my office. One that looks like real torches and lanterns. I just never took the time. But several of the light fixtures were in a "state of disrepair" now, so it might become an issue that I need to handle sooner rather than later.

I headed outside to inspect the lights myself. I spent about an hour looking at all the lights and decided that it was finally time to replace the lighting.

I'd started back to my office when I noticed a lovely young blonde woman sitting

at the bar, chatting with Curtis. It was Emily, and she was laughing at something Curtis said. He did have quite a charm about him. Curtis had a gruff-looking face with blondish hair that he kept cropped very short. He wore glasses and a goatee but was always clean-shaven beyond that. The guests loved Curtis and he loved the guests. That was always a good combination. I came up behind Emily and lightly cleared my throat for attention.

"Mind if I join you?"

She looked up, smiling as if we were old friends and she'd been expecting me. "Oh, no. Please, Sam, have a seat. Curtis and I were just chatting, and I had just ordered myself a sandwich." She swirled her drink, which looked to be a martini.

"Great! I'll have one, too. Two of whatever Emily is having, Curtis."

Curtis smiled a strange conspiratorial smile. "Yessiree, boss," and he swaggered away to fetch up our orders.

"I think Curtis likes me," Emily began. "You crushed his groove."

"Oh? I can't say as I've seen Curtis' groove before—maybe I should have stood back and watched." We both laughed and the image of Curtis hitting on her continued to amuse me.

"I'll agree; you are quite enchanting, so I can see how he might give you a little extra attention. So, what's a pretty lady like you doing at the bar like this in the middle of the day?"

She laughed lightly again. "Interesting choice of words, Sam. Really, I have nothing else to do. I came out here to relax, maybe have some fun and instead I find myself bored out of my mind. I work all week, sometimes six days a week. I take a few days every spring for myself to unwind, but I usually go to the Bahamas or Cozumel or somewhere touristy like that. This is the first year I just booked something, got in the car and left. I'm usually not alone..." Her voice trailed off, and she seemed to stop herself. "I know I told you it was a few days ago, but to be honest, I just booked the reservation with you the day before, which is probably why it wasn't in your system."

"That is possible—it usually takes a couple of days for us to get all the information in our system." Yeah, go for that small talk. Chicks love technical innkeeper stuff; it's a real turn-on. I read that in a Playmate's profile once.

"Oh, but listen to me. You really don't care what I do. You're just being the nice owner of the inn and listening to my rambling." She sighed, and her eyes caught mine again.

"No, really, I saw you in here and came in to see how you were doing.

How did your bubble bath go? I trust you enjoyed the wine and chocolate and had no further lighting issues?" I asked, with a clear image of how the bubbles would sit on her perky breasts and the warm water would caress and outline the valley between them. I stopped smiling quickly, before it got too creepy.

"No... I mean, yes." She stopped for a minute and continued thoughtfully.

"I mean the bubble bath was wonderful. The oils you have in the rooms are quite exquisite." Sandy chose all the bath amenities. "And no, I have not yet enjoyed the wine and chocolates. It seems so... I don't know... *desperate* to sit around and drink by yourself, don't you think?"

I wasn't really thinking of anything so much as imagining her rubbing oil down her firm calves and up the inner half of her supple thighs. Desperate? I somehow doubted this lovely young lady was desperate. I was desperate, but I wouldn't sit around eating chocolate and drinking wine by myself. I have Jack to keep me company, and he doesn't like chocolate.

"No, not at all. Having a nice glass of wine to help you relax and unwind, why not? That's why you're here." Curtis came back with two tuna salad sandwiches... I hate tuna. And the smile on his face betrayed that not only did

Curtis knows that, but he enjoyed retaliating for my presumptuousness. I guess I just assumed she had ordered anything but the one thing we had that I did not like.

"Thank you, Curtis," I said with a small sigh and a smile.

"Yes, thank you very much, Curtis," Emily offered with a warm smile.

Curtis smiled and retreated with a quiet laugh, only stopping for a moment to give me a look of smug satisfaction. Emily and I ate our sandwiches and chatted a bit more. I learned that she is 27 and a lawyer in Center City with a medium-sized law firm. She got her law degree from University of Pennsylvania and loved the city so much that she decided to stay. She has a condo in Center City in the Benjamin Franklin House and loves being close to the theater and Chinatown. We chatted for a couple of hours, had a few drinks… she stuck with the martinis and I began my Jack ritual, but added some soda to it so I didn't look like a complete lush.

Around 4, Natalie found me to let me know she was heading home to get ready for her guests. She frowned a bit when she heard Emily and I laughing, seemingly a bit intoxicated from our many cocktails.

"Sam, I'll see you tonight, right?"

"Oh, yeah… of course. I'll be there."

I had completely forgotten that Natalie had invited me to her Bible study group a couple of days ago—her attempt at saving me from myself. Maybe she was leading me down the path of righteousness or something like that. I said I would go; I didn't want to be rude or hurt her feelings. And heck, if they really had a pitcher of margaritas there, how bad could it be? But now, after my little run-in with Pastor Paul, I was a bit sheepish about going.

"What time was it again, Nat?"

"We start at 7 o'clock sharp." She stared at me for a good ten seconds, and I smiled and nodded.

"Seven, Sam."

"I got it, Nat, I got it."

She left, but didn't look terribly happy about our exchange.

Emily and I continued our drinking and chatting. We talked more about her career, how much she loved the beach and warm weather. I wondered if she was this open with everyone or if the martinis were prying her open a little bit. No matter—it was fun. And I still couldn't put my finger on what it was that drew me to her. Besides her killer ass and fantastic rack, of course.

"Sam, don't you have to go?" Emily pointed to the clock behind the bar. I hadn't even noticed the other guests come in for dinner at six. It was now almost seven.

"Oh, yeah, crap..." I gathered myself quickly and began to leave. "Hey,

Emily, wanna come?"

"Come? With you? Umm... Where are we going?"

"Bible study—Natalie, my front desk manager, hosts one every Saturday night. I've never gone before and would love to have some company. Maybe even give me an excuse to bail, if I need one."

"I don't... I don't think I should. It's not really my thing." All of a sudden, like a door, Emily was closed to me. Atheist, perhaps? Damn. I'd overstepped my bounds. Never mix religion and sexy breasts.

"I'm sorry, I was presumptuous, I just... I'm very sorry. I'll see you later.

Enjoy your evening." With that, I bolted out of the bar.

I didn't see Emily's reaction, but I did grab the bottle of Jack on my way
out of the office. Just what I needed: Some liquid fire for my belly... and head.

The good news was that Natalie's apartment was only a 10-minute walk from the inn. The bad news was that I spent an hour polishing off that bottle of
Jack, and that 10-minute walk took almost another hour. It was almost 9 when I stumbled up to Natalie's door and started banging. She opened the door, and her look of relief quickly dissipated into horror, then shock, then anger. She stepped outside and was so upset she could barely speak to me.

"I cannot believe it. You are two hours late, and drunk. I can't introduce you to the group, it's... it would be... embarrassing. What is wrong with you?

And why are you hitting on guests? Stay away from her, Sam—she's bad news."

I didn't respond, and she just looked at me with a hard disdain.

"Please, go—just go home."

With that, she turned around and shut the door without looking at me again.

"Screw you; I didn't want to come to this stupid thing anyway..." Then I heard the door click... Had it not been shut? Did she hear that? Dammit. I turned back around to knock on the door and apologize but thought better of it. I would just make it worse.

I stumbled back to the inn but took a detour into the bar. Several guests stared as I made my way behind the bar, looking for Jack. He usually didn't hide from me, but I was having a hard time finding him. Curtis came out.

"What are you doing?" he whispered. "Go to bed; you're already loaded."

Where the hell did he go?!

"Sam, seriously, get your skinny ass out of here before I have to haul it out myself." Jack! I grabbed the bottle, then looked at Curtis. "Screw you. Leave me alone."

I stumbled out of the bar into my office with my only buddy. Good ole

Jack. I didn't even get through half the bottle before I passed out face down on my desk.

What a great day.

March 9ᵗʰ

In the morning, my memory was a little bit fuzzy, so I called Natalie into my office to tell her I was giving her a 10% raise because of how valuable she was to me and how I couldn't run the inn without her. She just looked at me and quietly said, "Thank you, is that all?"

"Well, I guess so… I guess I was just expecting you to be a little more excited."

"Excited? Are you kidding? You think that after last night, you giving me a raise could excite me? Sam, you need help. I invited you over last night to reach out to you and show you I was your friend that I care about you and… and that I…"

She stopped here and fiddled with her hands a bit.

"Sam, I am having a really difficult time just watching you drink yourself to death. Sandy, Tyler, and Caitlyn would never have wanted this to happen to you.

And I… I just can't sit here and watch."

"Natalie," I began, "I know that our relationship is a bit deeper than just working together, but that is really none of your business. I appreciate your concern, but I will deal with my life and the loss of my family in any way I see fit."

I might as well have punched her in the stomach. Her face went white with shock. I thought she was about to cry. She obviously couldn't believe the words that just came out of my mouth... could I? None of her business? That simply was not true. I wanted her to care. I did.

"I... I don't know how much longer I can work here like this. I understand your position. I can't watch this happen to you. I'm sorry for intruding. If you need me, I'll be at the front desk—for now. I'll let you know what I decide to do."

And she was gone before I could do or say anything. What an idiot. She was probably the best person in my life, and I might as well have run her down with my car and said, "Oh gee, sorry." What an ass.

So I fired up the misery mix and poured myself a drink. And that's what I did for the rest of the day...

Oh how I wish, how I wish you were here...

March 10th

I awoke suddenly at 3:10 and saw that it was still dark out. My head was pounding over and over, like the surf at high tide pounding on the shore... in and out, over and over. My eyes blurrily fixated on something in front of the window. What, who was that? It was a person... a woman... I rubbed my eyes and could only see the glare of the desk lamp shining on the window, which overlooked the back garden behind the inn. It was eerily quiet—I'd left the Misery Mix playing, but it had stopped. The only sound was a light wind against the window... and there was that feeling again. The one from the cemetery, but it seemed that obvious no one was here. Well, except for that person I just saw when I woke up, that person who is no longer here.

That's when I saw it. At least, I think I saw something move out of the corner of my eye. There was something on the bookshelf, something that I don't remember being there before. I looked over at the books on the shelf just below the window, my eyes rested upon a folded piece of paper. Had that been there before? I hadn't cleaned my office in weeks, but there was never anything except books on that shelf. I picked up my head... slowly. My fixation with the mysterious paper helped to numb the pain in my head, but it was still there.

As I slowly got to my feet, I felt that the paper wasn't the only thing different in my office, but I couldn't place what else was wrong. I walked over to the bookshelf and stared at the paper. It seemed to mock me, to dare me to pick it up and open it. It beckoned me to read its contents and discover its mystery.

So I reached for the paper. It was a simple note, written in blue pen with familiar flowery handwriting:

> *You don't know what happened.*
> *You don't understand. They need Help.*
> *Only you can help.*

My eyes scanned the entire office. I felt like someone was messing with me—what happened, where? What don't I understand? What help? What was this note referring to? Who needed help? How did it get here? And why me? I didn't know, but my head hurt and I didn't know what to do at that moment.

Seems like I don't know much. Was this a sign that I should stop drinking or start praying? Maybe turn to God for help? I wasn't sure, but one shouldn't make rash decisions under duress. So I reached for Jack and took a nice long gulp from the bottle.

Then I noticed the door to my office was slightly open. I was sure that

Natalie closed it on her way out, but here it was, open. Who came in here? Who wrote me this note, and what did it all mean? I thought I recognized the handwriting. It looked a lot like Sandy's handwriting, but that was impossible. All of this was making my head hurt even more. Was it time to start praying?

Maybe I should give Pastor Paul a call.

I put the note in my pocket and opened the office door further. I made my way out to the lobby to find Natalie at the front desk. She looked at me; at first it was more of a glare, but she quickly softened when she saw the panicked expression on my face.

"Sam, what's wrong?"

I stared at her for a long moment, regaining a bit of composure.

"Were you in my office? While I was sleeping, did you come in my office?"

"Sleeping?" I could see the look of disbelief on her face. "No, after our"— she stumbled just a little—"meeting, I went home and then came back in to do my night shift at 10 as usual on Sundays. Why?"

"Did you see anyone come into my office?" I noted that my tone of voice was a little on the harsh side, and I should probably soften it up. I'm not mad at

Natalie—I think.

"No, Sam. What is going on? You're acting strange, even for you." Real nice, but true; it's just great when people know you better than you know yourself.

"Nothing. I... just... someone came in my office and moved something while I was asleep, that's all. It's nothing. I guess."

And what the hell did that mean? *Even for you*? As I turned to go to bed,

I could feel Natalie's stare on my back. Her pity, her condescension... At that moment, I hated her for it.

On the way to my cottage, I decided to take a walk around, just to make sure everything was okay around the inn. Okay, so that wasn't the true reason. I just needed to walk and think. As I made my way around the inn, I began to wonder what I was doing. What was I going to do? How long could I go on this way? Nothing was making sense; I couldn't even think of anything I wanted anymore. I stopped and looked out a window. My head didn't hurt quite as much as it had earlier. I rubbed face in my hands and then scratched my head.

"Time for bed, old man," I murmured to myself.

That's when I heard it, though I think I felt it as much as I heard it. It was soft, so soft it was barely audible. It was coming from down the hall. Crying... A woman was crying. I followed the muffled sounds of tears to the Jefferson Suite.

Emily was upset, and at 4 in the morning? Before I could think about what I was doing, I was knocking on the door.

"Emily, is everything alright? It's Sam."

The crying stopped. And there was only silence for what seemed like the longest time.

"Listen, if you need anything please, just..." and the door opened. Emily stood there, looking absolutely beautiful. She had on a powder-blue cashmere sweater that enhanced her emerald-green eyes and a dark blue skirt with no stockings. I barely even noticed that her eyes were swollen with tears. I just stared into them for a long moment. They had a hold on me again. She sniffled, and it brought me back.

"Why are you"—sniffle—"here?"—sniffle.

"I... I was just, well... to be honest, I was having a difficult night and decided to take a walk around the place before heading off to catch a couple of hours of sleep."

Honest? Yeah, that's what that was.

"And I heard you crying. I was concerned—is everything okay?"

What a stupid question. A pretty woman is crying and I'm asking her if everything is okay. She should just slam the door in my face for asking stupid questions. Instead, she stifled a cry and just shook her head.

"No," she whimpered and suppressed another cry. I wanted to hold her, to pretend that I could make whatever was wrong right again.

"Is there anything I can do?" I asked.

"I don't think so," she said simply and without any real emotion.

"Hey, I've got an idea. Why don't we go downstairs, I'll open the pub, and we can have a drink?"

"No, I don't think... I mean, I don't want to go downstairs. I don't want... I still have that bottle of wine, maybe... I mean, would you mind coming in and..."

She trailed off and looked down at her cute little toes.

"Sam, can I talk to you? I mean, really talk to you? I need to talk to someone... to you, I think." Her face was questioning and appealing to me for help, maybe even for answers. She looked away, and I knew that she wanted me to—no, needed me to—come in.

"Of course." She had already turned to retreat into her room, as if she knew I would say yes and follow. Was my lonely desperation that obvious? Or could she really read my mind? Either way, I followed her into her room quite willingly, trying not to get too close. I wasn't entirely sure I trusted myself alone in the room with her, considering my condition. I could see that she had already taken the bottle out and put it on the table, perhaps contemplating drinking it alone? I knew how she hated the idea of drinking alone.

Maybe she was anticipating someone else's arrival... mine, even? Dear Lord, I hope I am not that transparent.

And what am I thinking here? What is my motivation for coming in? I don't even know. Is it sex? Am I really considering taking advantage of a guest at my inn? A beautiful, sexy female guest who is clearly upset and vulnerable?

Or am I just so desperate for human interaction with someone who doesn't feel sorry for me? Or someone like Nat who is constantly judging me.

Maybe Natalie was right about my sudden fascination with Emily. Maybe it was wrong to be here and I should just walk back out the door. Just then, Emily bent over to pick up a pen off the floor. The sudden appearance of the soft valley of her breasts before me chased away the thoughts of Natalie and how wrong this was and ushered in a burgeoning erection.

As I did my best to think unsexy thoughts, I walked over to the cabinet in the corner of the room and took out two glasses. I retrieved the bottle opener from the basket and proceeded to open the bottle of merlot. Emily sat down in one of the high-back chairs in the sitting area of the suite, with her legs folded up underneath her. I could see the tops of her knees peeking out from underneath her skirt. I was so distracted I almost spilled the wine while pouring it into the glasses.

I walked over and handed her a glass. "For you, my lady." I offered her the wine with a smile. I sat down and sipped my wine, but she did not return my smile.

"So, what's the trouble tonight, darling?" What was that? Was I attempting some poor man's Valentino impression? Weak, even for me—I'm cheesy, but not usually this cheesy. What about her was making me act this way?

I looked over at what had previously been a warm, welcoming face, but tonight it was dark, troubled, and lost. She stared down into the dark, rich liquid and drank the red wine as if it were water to quench her thirst. She still hadn't looked at me since I sat down. And she appeared to hold the wine in her mouth for a long moment, savoring its rich warmth and welcoming flavor. I leaned forward, tried to look into her face and was about to speak when the words just shot out of her.

"I don't know where to begin or what to say. It's... I was..." She stopped herself, closed her eyes and took another drink, steeling herself to broach a subject that was apparently a sensitive and difficult one.

"I am married." The look of shock on my face was clear and instant.

"I mean, I was married for five years."

Okay, really, when I thought about it, it made sense. She probably could have been married for ten years but it hadn't really occurred to me.

"He... I loved him so much. He was..." Another drink, and her glass was empty. She continued to stare into it anyway. "I loved him so much..."

I got up, grabbed her glass, and brought it over to refill it. As I picked up the bottle, she began to cry again, this time loud and almost violently.

"Oh, why do you care? You don't even know me." She practically screamed through her tears. I stopped for a moment and then continued to pour.

Her loud cries turned into muffled sobs. I turned slowly, almost unsure of how to proceed. Was I doing something wrong? I was trying to behave myself and be helpful. Slowly, I walked back to the chair, where her blonde hair was softly bouncing with her sobs. I knelt down before her, placed my finger under her chin, and lifted it gently until her eyes met mine. She sniffled and looked right into my eyes. I handed her the glass and wiped the tears from her face with my other hand.

We stared at one another for a long moment, and I could see how much she was hurting as her eyes bore into me. They grabbed a hold of me again.

Suddenly I was speechless and had to remember to breathe. At that moment I wanted to touch her and make her feel safe, warm, and cared for. Wanted to press her face against my soul and let her know she wasn't alone. Because at least for tonight, she wasn't.

Finally, I found my voice as she continued to sob.

"Emily, I don't know what you are going through, but I'll sit here and listen.

For as long as you need to talk, you have someone here for you."

Her expression took on a look of wonder and disbelief.

"You... Why?" And she drank the entire glass in one gulp. How ladylike; maybe she'd belch in my face now. But her expression quickly went from disbelief to an almost self-satisfied look.

"Emily, I'm not sure exactly..." I began, but she cut me off.

"No, I know why you're here. You're just like him." Her mood had quickly gone from desperate sorrow to anger. Mental note: When coming to the aid of a crying woman, skip the wine.

"You..." she stammered for a second. "I know why you came in." Now she was repeating herself and I didn't like where this was going. "You just want to fuck me, isn't that it? We throw our bedroom eyes around, flirty smiles, a touch here and there, and you show up to my room in the middle of the night...

So now you think you can just waltz in here and I'll just drop my skirt to the floor and wrap my legs around you? Is that it?"

I stood up to face her and just stared at her, speechless, the shock evident on my face. I mean, the imagery was pretty erotic, but that's not exactly where my mind was at the moment. She stared back up at me, but I couldn't read the look on her face. My sudden movement had at the very least startled her, but I wasn't sure if her misplaced anger had abated. But I did know that I wasn't going to sit here and be attacked.

"Emily, maybe I should just go." I drank my wine and turned to leave. I got about halfway to the door when I felt her hand on my shoulder.

"Sam." Her voice was suddenly soft and quiet, barely audible, and I stopped. Knowing I shouldn't, I turned to face her.

"Emily, really, I can see you are upset and I'd like to help, but I guess being helpful is just something I'm not very good at."

"I know." She looked down at the floor and put her face in her hands. "I'm so sorry, that was wrong of me. I'm very upset and I'm not... I'm not thinking straight." She turned, walked back to the chair, and stood in front of it with her head down and back to me. The Jekyll and Hyde routine continued.

"Sam, I loved my husband. And he... he left me for another woman. Or maybe it was women; I don't even know."

Suddenly I had the urge to walk back and put my hands on her small shoulders that sagged in defeat.

"Emily, I'm so sorry…"

"Sam, I don't need pity. It was a while ago, and I… I thought it wouldn't hurt anymore, but tonight, I just… I can't seem to get a hold of myself… It is, or I mean, today would have been our anniversary. "

"Emily, I'm so sorry…"

My voice trailed off. I didn't know exactly how to finish that sentence without sounding cheap and condescending. I mean, who the hell am I to be consoling anyone with the way I handle—or avoid handling—things? Should I introduce her to Jack? I'm sure they've met before. Jack is very popular.

I could feel her shoulders slowly rise and fall under my hands. She stopped, drew in a deep breath, and held it for a long moment.

All at once she spun around, threw her arms around me, and pushed her lips up against mine in a violent kiss. Jekyll was back; or was it Hyde? Which one was the good one again? She held me tightly against her as she shoved her tongue deeply into my mouth, and I just stood there accepting her warm tongue in my mouth, shocked and confused until I finally pushed her away. Not sure what to do, I just stared down at her.

"Sam." She breathed heavily. "We both want this— you know that you do, and I'm telling you I want you." She pressed herself up against me, harder this time. I could feel her hands begin to make their way down the front of my shirt towards my pants. Her hands reached my belt and began to unfasten the button on my jeans when I grabbed her hand.

"Emily, you're upset; you just said yourself that you aren't thinking clearly."

"Sam, please," she said plainly, not pleading, "you want me, I want you; let

me take you into me and ease your pain… and mine." She took her hand back, stepped back just enough so I could see her begin to loosen her skirt.

"Emily, you are drunk!" I said forcefully.

Her demeanor instantly changed. She quickly took her hand away from the waist of her skirt and her face flushed. She looked like a wounded puppy as she slowly backed away from me.

"I'm sorry, I just felt… I was in the moment, and I really thought… Oh,

God, I am so embarrassed." She slumped down into the high-back chair again and covered her face with her hands.

"I can only imagine what you're thinking." No, I don't think she could imagine that my mind is pretty much blank right now, in spite of my obvious erection. Did this kind of back and forth constitute foreplay for me? How pathetic is that?

"I didn't invite you in to do that," she said with an even monotone.

I continued to stare down at her. As I stared at her sitting there looking defeated, I was unable to look away and unable to speak.

"Sam, say something. Say anything, but don't just stare at me like that…"

Her voice cracked slightly as her emotions started to bubble up again.

"I… don't… know what to say, Emily. I just don't know, I didn't expect this,

I didn't come in to sleep with you."

"When I found out that Scott was cheating on me, I was angry. I was hurt and all I wanted was to know why, and he couldn't tell me." She stood and walked to the table with some conviction, then picked up the wine bottle by its neck and looked out the window. She put it to her lips and took a big swig from the bottle. More ladylike behavior—that was kind of hot.

"Really, I don't... you don't have to explain yourself to me."

"Sam, you don't have to say anything—just sit and listen."

So I did. I sat down and listened, almost as if I couldn't get up and leave.

She had me, and I couldn't let go for that moment.

"I was so angry... I said I was going to go out and fuck all of his friends and anyone I could find with a big dick... but I didn't. He left me almost a year ago and before I could even grieve the loss of my marriage or even figure out how to file for divorce, he was dead and I didn't know what to do with that."

She walked back and sat down. "I still don't." She laughed sardonically.

"The only thing that I really know is that she was blonde. Wasn't I enough blonde for him?" She took another big drink from the bottle, and all I could think of was here we were, two people who had lost the loves of their lives... had the one person in the world that was supposed to always be there stolen from them, and by what? By whom? God? Fate? Cruel fate. At least Sandy wasn't sleeping with someone else... right?

"I knew this weekend was going to be hard for me, so I thought it would be good for me to get out... get away... so I came here. I thought it would help."

She paused and finished the bottle. She began to sway a little, wiped at her eyes, and finally flopped against the back of the chair.

"Sam," she slurred, "thank you for sitting here..." Her speech was slowing down; apparently the wine was starting to kick in.

"It's no trouble at all; I can listen any time." But I still couldn't get up. She was slumping into the chair with her blonde hair tossed forward onto her shoulders, her arms flopped over the arms of the chair and her legs spread slightly to keep her balanced. I was so drawn to her; I felt like a Weight Watchers deserter standing in front of a Chinese buffet fighting myself not to go inside.

"Yeah," she laughed, "maybe next time I'll keep my hand out of your pants."

I smiled, and we were quiet for a while. Emily's quiet moment seemed to allow the alcohol to really affect her, and she began to drift off. With her hand draped over her face, she looked like she had fallen asleep as the bottle trailed out of her slender fingers. Finally I was able to stand up and get out of the chair.

I jumped and caught the bottle before it fell to the floor and placed it on the table.

I walked back to the chair and gathered her slight frame into my arms, then carried her over to the bed and put her down.

"Sam..." her voice was soft and still slow and drawn out, "stay... lie with me? Please? No sex, just..."

We must be kindred spirits; she gets drunk and wants someone to lie in bed with her and not have sex, too. And before she could finish or I could answer, she passed out.

"Emily?" She didn't answer, so I turned out the light and shut the door softly behind myself. I made my way to my room, realizing that my headache was long gone but my head didn't feel any clearer. What was I supposed to do with this new information? Did it matter? Would I even see her again? I should make it a point to find her before she checks out tomorrow, make sure she's okay. A dead cheating husband... I wonder what happened. And what was that comment about not being sure if he was sleeping with more than one woman? It was an odd thing to say.

Maybe she could be that person I talk to and the shrink could go away... she's a lot prettier and probably a lot cheaper—even with the wine.

I finally made my way to the cottage, flopped into bed, and fell right to sleep.

Everything was happening in slow motion. I could see Sandy standing in front of me, pursing her lips and shaking her head. She was saying something, but I couldn't hear the words coming out of her mouth. Her eyes tore through me with anger and disappointment. What was it? Why was she so angry... what had I done? I don't know....

I can't think straight. She turns away from me and puts her head in her hands. She is still speaking, saying something, but now I can't even see her face. Then she spins and marches toward me, pointing a finger in my face and screaming. I know I'm saying something to her, but I don't know what it is; I'm mad and I can feel that I don't mean what I'm saying, but it comes out and her face is stricken...I might as well have smacked her. Every time she shakes her head and her blonde hair swings back and forth... Her eyes are closed, yet the tears still stream down her cheeks.

And before I knew what was happening, she was out the door with the kids in the car. And she was gone. I ran out the door after her and watched the taillights stream down the street.

March 10th (after sleep)

The sunlight finally roused me out of bed after eleven. The dream still haunted me. I couldn't hear what Sandy was saying, but I knew... I knew exactly what she said during that last fight. And I would never forget it. I had hurt her in a way a man should never hurt a woman... she loved me, and I struck out at her and said unthinkable things that night. There are some things that once said, can never be taken back... some words that can't be unsaid.

But how did the kids get in the car? She had already planned on leaving, even before the fight. It was crystal clear to me now. Check-out was at noon, and I wanted to try and catch Emily on her way out... talk to her, even just say goodbye. I felt like things were left incomplete... undone. I quickly showered and dressed and made it out to the lobby. Bonnie was at the front desk and helping a guest with something. I went behind the desk, nodding at Bonnie.

"Good morning, Mr. Shepard."

Bonnie was a cute teenager Natalie was mentoring at her church. She had asked me if she could hire her to work part time to help Bonnie earn money for a mission trip. I think they were going to New Orleans or Mississippi. Bonnie also did a good job and was great with the guests.

"It's Sam—please call me Sam, Bonnie. Mr. Shepard was my father."

Wow, did I just say that? How goofy can you be?

"Okay, Sam..." and Bonnie giggled a little as I quickly typed Emily Noble in the computer. Damn. Already checked out... and at eight. That was awfully early, especially after that late night and the wine.

"Bonnie, did you check Miss Noble out this morning?"

"No, Sam," I think she giggled again, "I didn't get here until nine. Natalie must have helped Miss Noble." Teenage girls sure giggled a lot.

"Thanks..." I shuffled out from behind the counter with a little extra weight in my step and decided to get a bite to eat in the pub. The pub was busy today, almost full, in fact. I could see that Curtis was hopping behind the bar... and who was sitting at the end of the bar with a cup of coffee in front of her but sweet

Emily. Why did I just call her sweet? She was kind of a bitch last night. Kind of? Actually, she was very bitchy when I was just trying to be helpful. It's almost as if when it comes to her, I don't have control over myself. Just like when Jack is around—no control.

I walked up behind her, and she looked over her shoulder at me.

"Hi," she offered quietly.

"Good morning; how are you feeling?" I sat next to her and her eyes found me again. And I couldn't look away, just for that long moment.

"My head hurts, and I really couldn't get any sleep. I thought I'd partake of some coffee before I hit the road back to Philly." She appeared increasingly uncomfortable, sitting there and looking at me. She stared down at her coffee and bit her lip.

"Sam…" she began hesitantly, "about last night." Ah, the classic words.

What a cliché. But since we didn't actually get all sweaty together, I found them slightly inappropriate.

"Emily," I interrupted, "I told you last night, I will be there to listen to you. I am here for you. Just always know that… and remember, you can call me."

She smiled a small smile… was it pleasant surprise, or that self-satisfied smile again?

"Thank you," she offered and took a sip of her coffee.

"Eat yet? I was going to have some breakfast." Curtis overheard that.

"Breakfast? You, Sam? You never eat breakfast," Curtis admonished.

"Yeah, well, I'm not usually up this early," I said with a sigh.

"Why up so early today?" asked Emily.

"Yeah, Sam, excellent question. We are all waiting to find out what has motivated you to grace us with your presence before noon," Curtis added with a sarcastic smile.

I shot Curtis an annoyed glance.

"I had something I forgot to give Emily, Curtis. Thank you very much."

Curtis returned my annoyance with playful contempt.

"Watch yourself there, pal. Don't make me toss you out of here. The owner doesn't like that sort of thing in here. And after your little display in here last night, I'm inclined to put your picture up behind the bar" — he gestured behind him — ""Do Not Serve.""

He laughed and went to help someone else with a mimosa. Emily joined him in the laugh and finished her coffee.

"No thanks, Sam, I have to get back. But I really enjoyed talking to you."

She fumbled in her purse for a minute and handed me a card.

"Call me... okay?" She looked at me hopefully and smiled.

I told her I would and gave her a small smile. She continued to smile as she glanced back at me and seemed to just disappear out the door of the pub. I must have been staring at the empty door for a moment too long.

"Sam, knock it off; she's gone, and you need to stay away from the likes of her," Curtis offered.

"Why would you say something like that? A beautiful, interesting woman like that might give me a much-needed diversion in my life." What a load of crap that was.

"There is something about her, Sam... something isn't quite right there."

"Curt, she lost her husband... she's... we have some things in common.

Maybe she's a little messed up. But she's in a way better place than I am, I'll tell you that much."

Curtis looked at me and frowned.

"No, that's not it."

"Then what?"

"I"—he stammered a bit—"I don't know, Sam, I don't know. But you need to trust me on this. I'm a bartender; I know people, and she's not good people.

Tear up that card; hope she never comes back here to stay. You should hope you never see her again. Something just isn't right there. It's like... she's got some bad mojo going on. Come on, have I ever given you bad advice before? I mean besides that thing with the stripper and her sister." He broke into a big smile.

He had a point. But really, the thing with the stripper and her sister wasn't really bad advice. The problem there was the execution of the plan. It's all a matter of perspective, really. Two hot girls, one guy, and four bottles of tequila.

What could go wrong?

The problem was, I didn't know what Curtis was talking about regarding

Emily, so I nodded at him and told him I'd see him later and left the pub. I couldn't stand for more conflict with Curtis... I need him on my side. And I know he was right to be worried about Emily. The last thing I need in my life right now is another woman. I really can't afford to have him against me... not like Natalie. I already hurt her and I can't stand it. I need them both; I just wish I could tell them. There's just too much loss in my life right now—I really need people around, even if no one wants to be around me.

March 11th

She was staring off into nothing. Her formerly beautiful blonde hair was unkempt and matted to her head as if it hadn't seen a brush in days. Her normally electric blue eyes were staring lifelessly out into the great nothingness of the wall. She stared off like she was waiting for something that wasn't there, but would be any moment now. Then, suddenly, she began to turn her head in a slow, deliberate movement. She stopped and fixed her gaze on me, and all at once, her eyes were alive. They were deep and pleading, begging me... but for what? What did she want? Slowly her lips began to move... to say something, but I couldn't hear what. I tried to speak, to tell her I couldn't hear her, but nothing came out. My mouth wouldn't move. Her lips were moving, forming a word over and over again... What was it?

Lady

I awoke suddenly, jumping up off the couch in my office. The pain in my head struck me hard in the temple. I got up and went to the bar to pour myself a drink. But there was a book sitting in front of Jack. I pushed it aside and grabbed Jack and a glass. Then I stopped cold.

I turned my head back to the book and stared. I could hear the phone ringing, but the outline of the book and the name were blindingly bright in my view. *The Portrait of a Lady* by Henry James. That was Sandy's favorite book. And as much as the ringing phone beckoned me and as much as my head hurt, all I could focus on was that book. I picked up the book and stared at the well-worn cover, still wondering what Sandy was trying to tell me. I opened the book and flipped through the pages quickly and learned nothing new. It was just a dream.

I poured myself that drink and tried to forget about the book and Sandy.

March 12th

When entire days just disappear like yesterday, it's hard to emerge and rejoin the world. There are messages waiting and people looking for me. They all want to know where I was, why they couldn't get me. The people closest to me know why, but they just hide their true feelings. Some people get angry or upset, some are concerned and have prejudged that I should be "seeing" someone for help. It is all so much fun. The biggest problem is that I just don't care enough to be polite to them most of the time. They leave messages urging me to call them—they need an approval on an order or a bill is overdue or something like that. And in the great big scheme of things, I just don't care.

I finally surfaced from my office and snuck through the inn to the cottage so I could grab a shower and get cleaned up. As I turned the corner near the lobby, Natalie was waiting for me.

"Sam, I wanted to apologize for the way I've been acting. I should be more sensitive to what you are going through. I'm sorry."

I stared for a minute... you know, deer in the headlights look... it actually took me a minute to remember our last tense exchange.

"Natalie, it's fine; it's okay. I'm sorry, too — let's just forget about it."

I tried to push past her, but she wouldn't let me pass.

"No, Sam, it's not alright. I'm your friend, end of story. If you fired me right here and right now, I'd still want to go have dinner with you." She stopped to breathe deeply, and all I could do was repeat my previous deer in the headlights expression.

"Sam, I want you to know I'm sorry for how I behaved."

I recovered myself somewhat and smiled at her.

"Nat, really, it's okay. I just need some more time — I need to get my head on." Had she just told me she wanted to have dinner with me? As I pondered this and watched her offer a small smile, I noticed a car in front of the inn. It was a black Lincoln Town Car, just sitting there idling.

"Nat, is that a guest's car?"

She turned. "No, I don't think so."

"Do you know if it's been here for long? It shouldn't just be sitting out there with the engine running like that."

"I saw it pull up about ten minutes ago, and it's been sitting there ever since. It was here earlier this morning but when I checked and it was gone; I just figured they were lost. Now it's back."

I stepped around Natalie and made my way toward the door. Just as I reached to push the door open, the driver threw it in drive, and the car squealed out of the circular driveway and out of sight. I stood at the door staring as it disappeared. Natalie came up behind me. "What's going on, Sam?"

"I don't know, Nat, but something about that car makes me feel uneasy.

Isn't that the same car that was parked across the street last week?"

"Ummm, well, I don't know. It could be, but black Lincolns are a dime a dozen around here. I think you're just being paranoid."

"I thought it was weed that made you paranoid, not whiskey." I tried a lame joke.

But she was right—we were ten minutes from the retiree capital of the

Northeast. There were more retirement communities in Ocean County, NJ, than in any other county north of Florida, and the old folks sure love their Lincolns and

Cadillacs. But it wasn't Lincolns and Cadillacs; it was a black Lincoln Town Car.

"Nat, I don't know—I feel like something is going on, and I'm the one left out in the cold. I'm having strange dreams, drunk blondes are throwing themselves at me, there are notes left in my office, and I'm hallucinating." I started to rub my forehead but noticed Natalie looking at me strangely.

"Blondes, Sam?"

With that I had to laugh out loud. "Yeah, Nat... blondes."

I had made a note of the Lincoln's license plate number as it tore away from the inn. I went back to my office and was about to pick up the phone to call the police when I decided to pick up *Portrait of a Lady* again. Something about that book... I'd missed something. So I opened it again and started reading:

Under certain circumstances there are few hours in life more agreeable than the hour dedicated to the ceremony known as afternoon tea.

I noticed the words "afternoon tea" had been underlined with pencil—did that mean something? Sandy had taken to going to the Country Cottage Tea Room in Beachwood for tea in the months before her death. She would go there to meet with her book club. Could this be something? *Portrait of a Lady* was the last book the book club was reading before she died. I had no idea, but I really hate reading, so I put the book down.

Feeling like I had learned something but not sure what it was, I picked up the phone and called Detective Sloane at the Point Pleasant Police Department.

"Sloane." Her voice was brisk and tough.

"Becky, long time no talk," I volleyed, trying to judge her mood. Becky was an old ex-girlfriend, and she was none too happy when Sandy and I got married.

She actually had a patrolman give our limo a ticket for illegally parking in front of

Saint Peters.

"Sam Shepard." She sighed wearily. "What can I do for you on this fine day?" she asked without a hint of helpfulness.

"Becky, I'm actually calling on some official business but hoping you could do an old friend a favor?" I asked hopefully.

"Well, if I recall correctly, it is you who owe me a favor. But go ahead, shoot—what do you need?" Her tone softened noticeably.

"Becky, there's been a suspicious-looking car around the inn lately. It was just here and I got the plates. I hoped maybe you could run it for me? See if anything interesting turns up?"

"I guess so—that's easy enough that I would do it even for you. Why are
you so interested in a black Lincoln? It's not like it's a bunch of rowdy kids in a
Camaro."

"I don't know. I've had an uneasy feeling lately, and this black Lincoln hanging around makes me feel like someone is watching me. Or maybe casing the inn. I'm worried someone might be casing the place, waiting to rip me off," I lied.

"Black Lincoln? Really? How can you be sure it's the same one? There are dozens around here." I could hear her smiling in disbelief at my seemingly ridiculous request.

"I know, I know, but I'm sure it's the same one." As I gave her the plate number, I felt even more certain that something was going on here, and this car had something to do with it. Becky told me she'd run a check on the plates and call me when she had something.

March 13th

My eyes fluttered open to see the moonlight shining brightly over the room. It was like someone was shining a spotlight into my bedroom. I had actually made it to my bed tonight and was only a little buzzed. I checked the clock and it was 2:55. I sat up, scratched my head, and looked around. I decided to get up and get a drink of water. I walked from the bathroom back to the bed; I sat back down, swung my legs into bed, said, "Good night, Sandy," and closed my eyes.

My eyes shot open and I couldn't move. I knew what I had seen. There was no denying it, and it chilled me to the bone. I had just seen Sandy lying in bed next to me.

She is lying right there with her back to me, I thought, her blonde hair splayed over her pillow and moonlight streaking over her purple nightgown. I was now lying with my back to her, and I didn't know what to do. Only a few inches from me was my dead wife.

After about thirty seconds, I realized I wasn't breathing. I took in a quick breath and slowly turned my head and shoulders to look, but she wasn't there. I sat up quickly, my breath was coming hard now and sweat was beading on my forehead. My head was now clear. It's amazing what kind of a buzz kill seeing your dead wife materialize next to you is.

I got up and went into the kitchen, looking for a glass and something to drink. The odd thing is that I don't keep any alcohol in the cottage. But I looked for it anyway. After ten minutes of searching for something I knew wasn't there, I gave up. I headed back to the bedroom and threw on a shirt to head over to the inn to grab Jack from my office.

I stepped out the cottage to walk across the grass and tripped over something. What the hell was that? Just a hat—someone must have dropped it, but normally there are lights on in the garden lawn area at night. Why weren't they on now? That was very strange. I stopped and looked around; only the lights from the street dimly lit the grass.

I started back towards the inn when a glare caught my eye. There it was on the other side of the street: A black Lincoln Town Car. I stood there and stared at it for maybe a second too long. I started to feel like my staring was obvious, so I continued walking into the inn. Probably just a car parked on the street. It didn't really mean anything.

But then that parked car revved its engine and pulled quickly away. I was feeling less and less paranoid and more like I was right. Someone *was* watching me.

A half an hour and a bottle of Jack later, I was passed out on the couch in my office. At least I wouldn't run into anyone dead while I was passed out.

March 14ᵗʰ

I was up and in the car before I thought about what I was doing or what time it was. Traveling down route 9, my mind raced through the past couple of days… from the book to the sightings of Sandy and the Lincoln. It all had to mean something. I pulled into the WaWa on the corner in the middle of Toms River and stared out into the water beyond the marina. My back started to send shots of pain up my spine. I sipped my cup of coffee, took some painkillers, and watched someone working on the outboard engine of their fishing boat.

At this spot, the river began to open up to its widest point before it spilled out into Barnegat Bay and then flowed into the Atlantic. The sun had come up and was shimmering on the river. It was still cold out, but it was a beautiful sight. Springtime was on its way. I stood there, staring, not really sure why I was here. Then I hopped back in the Chevelle and fired up the engine, staring out the windshield, knowing exactly where I was going.

Ten minutes later, I pulled onto the concrete squares of the old formation blocks and killed the engine. I guess I could have pulled forward into the parking lot, but I always wanted to park on the blocks. So I did—and enjoyed it

Sands of Time by Bruce A. Sarte

thoroughly. I know; it was kind of a stupid, rebellious thing. But I deserved it for having spent so much time with my face pressed against that cold concrete doing push-ups. I got out of the Chevelle and walked around the side of Farragut Hall, past where the Capstan once stood, and looked out over the waterfront where Sandy and I first met.

I was 15 years old and a sophomore second-year cadet trying to learn how to sail. The only problem was, I seemed to like to be *in* the water more than *on* the water. And given that it was late in October, *in* the water was not somewhere you wanted to be. I was making a weak attempt at bringing the boat into the dock and not really having much success. I threw a line in, trying to hook it around the pier, when she came up to the dock and grabbed the line. I looked up and saw her blonde hair blowing in her face, and she pulled me in. And I was hooked on her as much as my boat was to the dock.

She was the dock master's daughter, so I quickly learned how to sail—and sail well. I spent every minute I could down at the waterfront; Sandy and I became very close very quickly. Before I knew it, the waterfront was closed for the winter and she was my date at the Winter Semi-Formal dance. I remember it like yesterday: She wore a black gown that was off the shoulder and enhanced her blossoming breasts with shimmering sequins. It was on those docks, on that night that we sat on the deck of an old boat, staring out at the river with the reflection of the harvest moon on the water. As I leaned in and kissed her lips softly for the very first time, I could see that same image of the moon in her blue eyes. I'll never forget that sight as long as I live.

I turned around and looked at Farragut Hall, windows boarded up, porch rotting and in paint peeling from the wood around the windows. I walked up the steps and pushed aside the yellow "DO NOT CROSS" warning tape that failed miserably in its mission to keep me off the decrepit porch. I walked around to the football field side of the porch and stared off at what was once the site of many sunny Saturday games, and some not-so-sunny ones. So many days of running around the track with a Springfield .22 caliber rifle raised over my head, Sandy and her friends watching from behind the gates and giggling at us poor losers. Suddenly, there was a loud bang from inside the building, and it made me jump almost out of my shoes. What was that, and where did it come from?

There couldn't be anyone inside, could there? The windows were all boarded up, doors chained and padlocked shut, but I was sure I'd heard something.

I walked to the side door and tried to look in the small windowpanes that weren't boarded up, but couldn't see anything inside. I pulled on the door; it was locked tight. I quickly ran around to the main doors of the building and pulled them, too, but they were locked as well as chained. So I turned around, walked down the front steps of the porch, and turned to face the building. The windows on the second floor were not boarded as the first floor's were, and many of them were broken. It seemed possible that someone could have found their way up onto the roof of the porch and made their way into the building through one of the windows.

"Hello," I yelled out and walked around to the north side of the building, where the old entrance to the naval science office and museum had once been.

I found that door not completely closed. I stepped down the three steps to the door and pulled hard. The top came away from the frame, but it appeared to be held in place by something from inside. I yanked harder, but it didn't give any more.

I tried to look inside and yelled, "Hello, is anyone in there?" but there was no response. Still, I wondered, was there something—or someone—in there? It was almost as if I could sense someone's presence but not see or hear him or her. I stepped back and gave the door a kick with the heel of my boot. It rattled and shook a bit but didn't seem to open further. So I kicked it again—what the hell, I thought. Then I gave up, walked back up the steps, and turned back toward the parking lot near the formation blocks. I got about three steps and was stopped in my tracks by a sloppy, overweight Pine Beach police officer doing his best to look tough.

"Sir, what did that door do to you for you to be kicking it like that?" He looked at me with contemptuous, mocking eyes.

"I... ah," I stumbled, not really knowing what to say. Now I really just wanted to leave.

"Sir, tell me. What is the nature of your business here?"

"Ahhh, no, well, I..." I continued to fumble for words, "I am an alumni of the school, and I was, umm, you know, just reminiscing a little. Checking out the old place. You know?"

The officer looked at me for a long moment but didn't seem sympathetic to my pathetic story.

"Sir, can I see some ID?"

"Of course." I reached into my jeans to get my wallet and driver's license out. After I handed it to him, he looked at it and back at me and smiled.

"You're Sam Shepard the race car driver, aren't you?"

I smiled, hoping I'd be able to get a little lenience from the cop now that he recognized me. "Yes, I am."

"Big fan, Mr. Shepard, but I am going to have to ask you to vacate the premises now—this is private property, and the owners don't really like folks poking around."

"Oh, yes, Officer, I understand." I looked at him, trying to decide if I should tell him about what I'd heard in the old building now that we'd made a connection.

I quickly decided that I'd keep it to myself for now, but I might need this guy later.

I took my license back from the officer. I began to walk toward the formation blocks, and I looked back toward the building. As I turned back toward the blocks, I saw something move and stopped. I glanced back around and looked at the last window before the fire escape stairs. I was sure I saw something move there.

"Officer," I turned to him, "does anyone come around here at all?"

He drew in a deep breath. "No, not really. Mostly just people like yourself who come back to mull over the good times, ya know what I mean, when they were young and had all those pretty little local girls hanging all over them."

He added a rich belly laugh and a wink to the last part.

"Oh, hey," I added, as if I'd just thought of it, "do you know who owns the property now?"

He looked thoughtful for a moment, or at least as thoughtful as he could manage.

"Well, I know its some folks from out of town, but can't recall the name right offhand. Why you so interested?"

My mind raced for a minute, trying to make up something that sounded plausible.

"I, um, am interested in buying the place, renovating it, you know. Give the old place a nice overhaul and restore it to its former glory," I lied through my teeth with a huge grin on my face, trying to sell it.

"Oh, I don't know, you could always go look it up at the library or call a real estate agent—they might know how to contact the owner." He looked back toward the building and then back to me. I looked past him and there it was again—something moved in that window by the fire escape. Was it a face? Was it blonde hair? It seemed like a blonde woman trying to sneak a look without being seen. Who was she? Probably just some kids messing around, trying to hide from the police. But something told me no, that this was more than that. Of course, it could have just been my mind showing me things that I wanted to see.

"Haven't had much interest in the old place since it closed. It'd be nice to see it alive again."

I walked to my car and got in, taking one last look at the campus.

Something is going on here, I thought, and it has something to do with Sandy. But what?

I pulled off the campus and drove through Pine Beach down Riverside

Drive, along the river and into Beachwood, until I got to the Beachwood

Community Center. I pulled into the parking lot of the empty, weatherworn blue building. The doors were still boarded up for the winter but would soon be open full of people getting their beach passes so they could swim, go boating, or just lie on the beach and get a tan.

I got out of the car and shut the door, the sound of the door slamming lost in the lapping of the river against the shore. I was drawn onto the beach by the river. I felt like it was calling my name, beckoning me to come to it. I kicked my shoes off and felt my feet hit the cool sand. I stopped, staring out over the water, seeing the houses on the other side standing in a stoic silence. I bent down and took a handful of the sand and let it slowly run through my fingers. I watched as the wind caught the grains of sand and took them wherever it pleased, though the end result put the sand back where it belonged. A different location, but still on the beach with the rest of the sand. It seemed like a pretty good metaphor for my life: Torn away from what was familiar and comfortable and put back into something that in appearance was very similar, but in actuality very different.

I still didn't have a firm grasp on how Farragut and the river related to

Sandy and the accident—in fact, I didn't even have a real clue as to exactly what

had happened. But I did know that they were related, and that Sandy and the

kids' death was not what it seemed.

Back in my car and free of my morose moment on the beach, I made my

way onto Route 9 and over to the Country Cottage Tea Room. It was almost 11, and as I remembered from when Sandy used to come down here, the tearoom didn't open until 11. I parked the car in front and went to get out but stopped when I noticed an orange sign taped to the entrance. I quickly got out of the car, and my cell phone started to ring a 215 number—Philadelphia. Who could it be, calling me at this time from Philadelphia?

"Sam here."

"Sam? Oh, good, I am so glad I got you." Her voice came through the phone like warm honey.

"Emily? How…" I began as I remember giving her my card with my cell number on it.

"Emily, what's up?"

"Sam, I wanted to call and make sure you were going to be around this weekend; I thought… maybe…" she trailed off. "Well, maybe I would come down this weekend and we could spend some time together?" she finished with a pound of hope and an ounce of doubt. I was a little flabbergasted and didn't know how to respond. I was quiet a little too long.

"Oh," Emily stammered, "I… I didn't mean to seem so… Oh, I am so embarrassed."

"Emily, no", I interjected quickly, "I'm just—I'm in the middle of something right now, and I was surprised to hear from you."

"I'm sorry, Sam. I really just wanted to see you again. Maybe talk a little, you know, while sober this time?"

I laughed a little, but it felt uncomfortable, a bit forced for some reason.

"I can't promise anything about being sober, but I would love to see you again. I'm sorry for my reaction—I was just a little surprised. I didn't expect to hear from you. Just come down tomorrow night and we'll go out and have dinner, maybe check out the boardwalk. It's the weekend— why not have a good time? What do you think?"

"Really?" she answered with excitement in her voice. "Okay, then I will see you tomorrow around 5? Any chance I can get the Jefferson again?"

"Well, I don't know," I chided. "I think I know someone who can arrange it.

Let me make a few calls, and you just show up," I replied, laughing at the same time. "I'll see you then."

"Okay, Sam," she said, and I could hear the smile on her face. "See you then." And her voice was gone.

I took a long look at my cell phone and smiled as I put it back in my pocket. I guess I have a date. Things were looking up.

I began walking to the tearoom again to read the orange sign in the window.

"CLOSED UNTIL FURTHER NOTICE"

Really? This couldn't be right. I pressed my face to the window to try and see inside. It was dark, and I could see the tables and chairs just like you would expect to see in a tea room. In the back corner was a long oval table that resembled a coffee table with a couch and high-back chairs surrounding it. I looked over at the counter, but no one seemed to be inside. I banged on the glass.

"Hello! Anyone inside?"

No answer. So I pounded on the glass again.

"Hello..." this time much quieter. I didn't expect a response. There was dust on the tables. The place had been closed for some time.

I walked around the back of the building and stopped dead in my tracks. I couldn't believe what I was seeing. I had my cell phone in my hand and was calling Becky before I knew what I was doing.

"Sloane here."

"Becky—it's Sam," I blurted out breathlessly.

"Hey, Sammy boy," she replied with mock enthusiasm. "I'm sorry, I just haven't had a chance to look into the Lincoln thing. I'll..." I cut her off.

"Becky, I'm staring at it. I am standing behind the Country Cottage Tea

Room, staring at that black Lincoln Town Car."

"Now, Sam, you can't go around following people. You could get in trouble and it's just not very nice, and I know how much you care about other people's feelings." She continued in her mocking tone.

"No, Becky, you don't understand. I came to the tea room and it was just here."

"Uh, Sam. You are right, I don't understand. You went out for tea—and don't worry, I won't tell anyone, so that shouldn't jeopardize your manhood—and you saw a Lincoln Town Car that was near your inn. I am very confused..."

"No, Becky..." She cut me off.

"Very confused as to why I give a shit, Sam. I will run the plates for you, but that's it. I shouldn't even do that, you cheating bastard." Her voice began to waiver. "This is not a police matter. I'm doing you a favor, so just get off my back and leave those poor old people and their Lincoln alone. And know this,

Sam: I don't give a shit." I winced as I heard the receiver clatter before the line went dead. I never realized how much I hurt her. But I couldn't worry about Becky right now. I was standing behind the tearoom that Sandy used to go to, staring at a car that has been stalking me for the past month. I went to the back door and started banging and yelling.

"Open this door! I know you're in there—open up!"

Nothing. No sound, no movement, no sign other than the car that anyone was here. I walked over to the car and tried the driver's side door handle. It was unlocked. I opened the door and looked inside. There was nothing in the car— except, sitting on the black leather of the passenger's seat, a book.

It was *Portrait of a Lady*.

I picked up the book and opened it. It had a name in the upper left corner of the book cover. Emily. The name couldn't mean anything, could it? It had to be a coincidence. There were millions of Emilys in the world. Had to be hundreds just in the area.

This was too much. First the car around the inn, then the book in my office, now the car at the tea room with the book and the name Emily in it. I didn't know what to make of it, but it was too much to be a simple coincidence.

I rifled around in the back and found nothing there. Now, I knew I had to search the entire car. First, I got out and looked around to see if anyone was watching. Seeing no one, I popped the trunk and starting rifling through the contents. There was an emergency kit, some empty shopping bags, and a suitcase. I looked at the brown Samsonite suitcase for a long moment. *Should I open it?* Before I completed the thought, I had the suitcase popped open. It seemed empty, except for a single picture at the bottom. I reached in and took the picture, letting the suitcase fall shut.

It was a picture of a group of women sitting around a table. There were two blonde women, three brunettes, and a redhead. They all looked so young, maybe in their mid to late twenties. The picture appeared to be taken from across the room—and I had seen this room before. I dropped the suitcase, walked around the front of the building, and peered into the tea room one more time, searching for it. There it was. The very same oval table in the picture.

And there she was in the picture, sitting at that table. Her head thrown slightly back, one hand to her chest, the other with a cup in it, mouth open in the middle of an animated laugh. She had her blonde hair up on her head in a loose bun with chopsticks through it. She looked so young, younger than I remembered. When was this taken? What the hell was this? I flipped the picture over to look at the back. Written in what looked like dark red ink was the phrase, "find me." I grabbed the door and began shaking it furiously. Having no idea why I'd bothered with that, I stopped and ran around the back again to go through that car for anything I might have missed, for another clue that would lead me to whatever Sandy was trying to tell me.

Again, I stopped dead in my tracks as I turned the corner.

This time, I left my cell phone in my pocket.

The black Lincoln Town Car was gone.

Back at the inn, things were pretty busy. It was mostly local people coming in and out of the lobby area on their way to the pub. We had a few guests staying at the inn through the week, but the rooms would fill up later tonight when the weekend guests checked in. I was making my way through the lobby and the human traffic when Natalie came up from behind me.

"Sam?" she called loud enough to get my attention, and I stopped.

"Nat, what's up?"

She looked me up and down and then struck a questioning posture, her dark blue eyes boring into me.

"Sam? Did you just come in from outside?"

"That is the direction I came from. Why?"

"Oh, nothing." She smiled a little. "Just glad to see that you are up and about before lunch is all." It was actually after noon, but her point was made.

"Well, that's nice of you. What's going on? I was going to my office to check on our weekend reservations."

"Really?" Her face brightened even more. I guess I was just full of surprises today.

"Yes, really. Emily wants to come back and stay tomorrow night. I was going to see if there was room in the Jefferson."

"Oh." Her expression darkened, and she frowned slightly. Then her face suddenly morphed into a crooked smile. "Sorry, Sam," she started slowly and picked up her pace, "we are booked solid this weekend. There's some reunion in Point this weekend. I guess Emily will have to stay home." Her smile betrayed her inner glee about Emily not coming.

"Oh, okay. Well, I guess we'll have to figure something out. I have to run.

Gotta make some phone calls. See ya later."

As I walked away toward my office, I heard Natalie mumble, "We?"

I found my way into my office and the disaster I referred to as my desk. It was almost one o'clock and Jack was sitting there staring at me, making me feel guilty for not even looking his way today. Maybe it was because I'm a creature of habit or maybe because I actually needed it; who knows the real reason at this point—I sure didn't. Still, I opened the bottle and released the warm brown liquid into the dirty rocks glass on my desk. I stared at it for a long minute, not sure why I had poured it. And before I could get too involved in my thought process, I downed the entire glass in one gulp.

Feel the burn.

As I poured another drink, I began to think about what I needed to do next.

What was my next step? How did I decipher this new information? What did the picture mean? And what was going on at the school? I didn't know, but I was sure they were related. It was too much like someone knew I was going to be there and left those things for me to discover.

I brought the glass to my lips and was about to indulge in another scalding

of my esophagus when the phone rang. I stared at it for a long moment, deciding whether to pick it up or down the Jack first. It rang at me again. I quickly downed the Jack and picked up the receiver.

"Sam Shepard here."

No response.

"Hello? Anyone there?" But I could tell someone was there—I couldn't hear them breathing, but I could sense them.

"Hello? I know you are there." I was getting a little annoyed. The Caller

ID showed Unknown.

"Okay, thanks for calling." I was about to hang up when I heard the voice.

Weak but familiar, it seemed to scratch its way out of the phone and into my ear.

"You can't save me."

My heart stopped and my breathing ceased.

"You can still save them." She was struggling to get the words out.

"Sandy?"

"Sam, save them."

And the line went dead. I almost fell out of my chair. I looked at the bottle

of Jack and quickly poured another drink, and downed it. Then I dialed Becky.

"Sloane here," she answered lazily.

"Becky, don't hang up; I need help."

"Sam, I was going to call you—the information on your Lincoln is back.

What's the big emergency over there?"

I stopped for a second and processed that information, deciding I needed to know where that phone call came from more than I needed to know about the Lincoln right now.

"Great, but this is more important. Someone just called me and pretended to be Sandy."

"Really?" she sounded skeptical. "How many drinks have you had today Sam?"

"Drinks? You think I'm drunk?" Dumb question. "I need you to find out where the last call to my office came from. The call was direct to my office, not through the front desk, so the person, whoever it was, knows my direct phone number."

"I understand how upsetting a cruel joke like someone calling pretending to be your dead wife can be, but I can't just run traces on prank calls."

"Don't you understand? She called me directly... on my phone... she said

I can save them."

"What do you mean *them*? Who was the person referring to?" Becky still didn't believe it was Sandy. Did I?

"The kids, Tyler and Caitlyn. They are still alive, and I need to know where they are. The place that phone call came from is my only lead."

"So let me get this straight. Someone called you, a woman who sounded like Sandy, and told you that Tyler and Caitlyn are still alive? Specifically? She mentioned them by name?"

"Well..." I stammered, "not exactly, but that's what she meant, and I know it was Sandy. I know my wife's voice when I hear it. And you hung up on me before I could tell you about the picture of Sandy I found at the Country Cottage

Tea Room. If they are all still alive, we need to find them. Now!"

Becky was quiet for a long moment, and I could practically hear her rubbing her eyes before she responded.

"Picture?"

"Yes, in the trunk of the black Lincoln."

"The Lincoln? You were *in* the Lincoln? Sam, you need to stay away from that Lincoln. That Lincoln is bad news...."

"Becky, I know its bad news; I've been trying to tell you there was something wrong about that car and it was parked behind the tea room. I thought it was too coincidental that I went to check out the tea room and the

Lincoln just happened to be there, so I checked it out. And I'm starting to think

Sandy has been trying to get my attention for the past week. I..." I started to stammer a little as my emotions bubbled up. "I've seen her in my dreams, I thought I saw her here in the inn, and then the other night I saw her in bed. And the note..."

Becky sighed audibly.

"Sam, I am going to forget the last part of what you said and tell you I do not believe for one minute that Sandy, Tyler, or Caitlyn are still alive. I saw the wreckage from the accident; I was on the scene. They could not have survived.

I'm sorry, Sam, but it's the truth. And next, I will tell you how sorry I am that someone is screwing with you like this. Finally, I will tell you that I will run a trace on your phone because based on what you have told me and the

Lincoln sightings, it is possible that you and Sandy might be mixed up with the Khayman clan."

Wait, what was she trying to say? That we were mixed up with the Khaymans?

"And Sam, if I find out you are mixed up with the Khaymans, I'll take you down. Old friendship or no old friendship."

"Becky, why would you think we were mixed up with the Khaymans?" I asked quietly.

"Because that black Lincoln is registered to Maxwell Khayman."

My mouth fell open. Maxwell Khayman was the Jersey Shore's main organized crime boss. He ran the strip clubs, drug trade, and prostitution ring.

But what did that have to do with me?

"I have nothing to do with Khayman, and neither does Sandy." But all of a sudden, I wasn't so sure.

"Sam, I will run the trace. But for now, stay away from that Lincoln." Then she hung up the phone. Didn't she know how to say goodbye?

This time, I skipped the glass and began drinking straight from the bottle.

I got up and went to the bar.

"Curtis!" I yelled when I didn't see him. People stared at the half-drunk guy yelling in the middle of the bar. Oh, wait, that's me. I walked behind the bar and went in the back.

"Sam, you drunk again? You know where the Jack is if you're out—you don't need me," Curtis said while openly laughing at me.

"Not yet, but I'm almost there. That's not why I'm here. I have plenty of

Jack in my office." I stopped and stared at him for a minute. He stared back.

"What do you want, then?"

"You know that guy you know? The real estate guy? Can you get me his number?"

"Yeah, I have his card in my wallet. Bob Hoskins." He fished the card out of his wallet and handed it to me. "Call him, he's good. Looking to sell the inn?

Buy a place in the Hamptons?"

"No, I need to find out where Sandy is." And with that, I walked out.

I can only imagine the look on his face and what was going through his mind. But it was the truth.

So much was happening so fast, and I knew the school was at the heart of

it all. When I got back to my office, I picked up the phone to call Bob.

Dammit. Voice mail.

"Hi, Bob, this is Sam Shepard. I need to know who owns the old Admiral

Farragut site in Pine Beach and how much they are asking. I want to buy it.

Call me back as soon as possible—it's urgent." I left my number, hung up, and

spent the rest of the afternoon with Dr. Daniels.

March 15th

The sound of the door clicking shut jolted me awake. I lifted my head from my desk and regretted it after feeling the thunder behind my eyes. I quickly checked the clock: 1:22. It was dark in my office except for the glaring of the red numbers on the digital alarm clock. I got up, crossed my office to the door, and swung it open. I sprung out from my office and jumped into the lobby about ten feet, looking around like a mad man. The hand on my shoulder made me jump and whirl around violently.

"Sam!" Natalie jumped back and put her hand to her chest.

"My God, Natalie, don't do that!"

She was breathing heavily. I must have scared her.

"Sam, I'm sorry. I didn't mean to... Are you alright?"

"Yeah, I'm okay. Did you see anyone in my office?"

"Yes—you. I was checking to see if you were still in there; did I wake you? I saw you in there sleeping at your desk and tried to be quiet, but I guess I wasn't as quiet as I thought I was. I am so sorry." And she did look very sorry. Cute, but sorry.

"It's alright, Nat. I thought... I'm just a little bit jumpy. I had a very disconcerting day, and my head hurts. I think I just need to go to bed." I put my hand to my forehead, pretending to feel the pain in my head with my hand.

"Do you need anything? Do you want me to help you back to your room?"

I stopped and thought about this for a moment. I looked at her dark hair resting lightly on the sheer white blouse open to her midriff, exposing the soft valley between her pert breasts that were covered by a blue shirt underneath. I imagined unbuttoning the blouse and letting it drop the floor. Lifting her arms up above her head and pulling the silk blue shirt off of her, revealing her soft lace bra while she gazed up into my eyes. My little daydream was interrupted by the phone ringing at the front desk.

"No, Nat. I'll be okay."

"Okay, Sam. I need to get that." And I watched her slim body move quickly as she darted off to answer the phone. And I was off to my bedroom in the cottage.

The night was dark and my head was cloudy. I walked through the courtyard and entered the cottage. It was pitch dark, with only the faintest light seeping in through the window into the living room. I slowly made my way through the living room, careful not to bump into the table or desk. I stopped just before exiting the living room. Was someone here? I could sense something, but I didn't know what it was. I couldn't hear breathing or sense movement. It was almost as if a corpse were in the room with me.

I looked around again, making sure to get a good look at the room without turning on the light. My eyes were keenly adjusting to the darkness. I didn't see anyone, so I moved on into the bedroom. I crossed the room and pulled my shirt off over my head. I dropped it on the floor and froze.

I wasn't breathing again.

Standing there, on the other side of my bed, was Sandy. She was cloaked in a dark robe, her skin pale as moonlight and lips red as burgundy wine.

Her eyes were open, but she wasn't looking directly at me. Instead, she was focused on the bed.

I didn't know what to feel or how to react.

"Sandy?"

"I know you were there today," she hissed with some difficulty. Was she having trouble breathing? Something seemed wrong with her. Could be that she was supposed to be dead. "Go back. Save them. I am gone and cannot be saved. My fate is sealed, but theirs is not. You can save them."

I still didn't know how to react to what I was seeing. Were my eyes—and ears—playing tricks on me? She lifted her head and stared right through me, her eyes black as night. My mouth fell open in shock and fear; I had never seen anything quite like it before. She lifted her hand toward me, not reaching for me but pointing at me. Then everything went black.

I awoke several hours later. It was still dark, but I couldn't see my clock.

Somehow, I was in bed. I didn't remember how I got there. But I remembered seeing Sandy.

But now she was gone. I sat up in bed and searched the room. I got up and ran into the living room; she was definitely not here. Had she been here at all? Did I imagine her? How drunk had I been? I made it to the cottage on my own, but maybe I should have brought Natalie back with me. Then she would have seen Sandy, too. Or would she have? And what if she didn't? Would I have tried to get Natalie into bed again? That would have been bad.

I looked out my bedroom window. The sun was just starting to show itself over the horizon. I surely wasn't going to get any more sleep after the excitement. I quickly showered and dressed. On my way out the door, I locked it— something I never did. The cottage was situated behind the inn in such a way that you had to either scale the fence behind the cottage or come in through the inn, so I never really worried about it. But after last night; it was so real— she was so real—that I locked the door. I think I need to stop visiting with Jack so much. He's making things a little less clear these days. Maybe I need some divine intervention.

The inn was very busy today—Natalie was right. The lobby was packed with people milling in and out. It was only a little after 7, and they were already heading into the pub for breakfast or out the door to enjoy the sunny day. I made my way through the lobby, into my office, and dropped myself behind my desk. I spent some time trying to get my mind off what I'd seen last night by paying some bills and ordering some cleaning supplies and linens online. But nothing could get that vision out of my head.

After a couple hours of failing to get the disturbing images out of the forefront of my mind, I gave in. I picked up the phone and dialed the number that had been pressing itself into my consciousness since I woke up.

"Blessed Morning, Pastor Paul here," came his upbeat and cheery voice.

"Pastor, it's Sam Shepard," I replied almost inaudibly.

"Sam, how are you? I've been praying for the Lord to guide you these past days. What brings you to call me this morning?"

"Pastor," I began with some difficulty, "I have…" I trailed off, finding the right words difficult. "I have been seeing things lately."

"Hmmm." I could hear the contemplation in his voice. "What sort of things?"

"Things… people…" I took a deep breath. "People who aren't there.

They can't be there." I finished with some anticipation hanging on the end.

He was quiet for a moment, and I could almost hear his disbelief.

"Would these be people I might know?"

"Pastor," I began quickly this time, "I think… I mean, do you have time to see me today?"

"Why, Sam, I always make time; when did you want to come by?"

"How about now?"

He laughed and responded confidently, "Sam, come on by, I'll shift a few things around."

I hung up the phone and was out the door and in the Chevelle in a matter of minutes. The muscle car's engine roared to life, and I gunned it onto the street to the church.

I stared at the deep mahogany of Pastor Paul's door before knocking.

He's going to sign me up for AA, I know it, I thought. I knocked on the door and waited for the pastor to call me in. I entered with a sheepish smile on my face, and before saying anything else, I apologized.

"Pastor, first I wanted to apologize for that night in the cemetery. It was completely out of line, and I am embarrassed by the whole incident."

"Sam, please, sit. If you had offended me, which you did not, the Lord says all is forgiven. How can I say any differently?" He adopted a big smile, rising from behind his desk to take the chair across from mine.

"So tell me, Sam, what has brought you to my office today? What are you seeing that has you so disturbed?"

I concentrated my eyes firmly on the leg of his chair and mustered everything I had within me to answer his question.

"Sandy," I said evenly and simply. "I have seen Sandy. And not just once;

I've seen her twice." He regarded me with a note of seriousness. "Pastor, she was as real as you are to me right now. She was lying in bed the other night, I swear it! I saw her as I went to get in bed, and I laid there for a minute, not sure what to do, but when I looked back again, she wasn't there!" It was all spilling out of me like water from an opened dam. The pastor held up a hand to stop me.

"Whoa, Sam, slow down." He leaned forward and placed his hand on my leg. "You saw her, then she was gone. It was simply your mind playing tricks on you, showing you what, in your heart, you wanted to see." I sat there, slowly shaking my head back and forth as the pastor continued, "I know how much you miss her and the children, and so does God."

"Pastor, you don't understand." I continued to shake my head. "She called me; I know it was her on the phone and... I saw her again last night." His expression continued to have a comforting air about it. Then I went on. "She spoke to me." He stopped smiling.

"Spoke to you?"

"Yes."

"What did she say?"

"She told me that she was gone but that they could be saved, and that she knew I had been there today."

"Been there? Been where, and who do you think she meant could be saved?"

"Pastor, isn't it obvious?"

He stared at me blankly for a moment, playing into my dementia.

"Tyler and Caitlyn. They're still alive."

His demeanor became very serious. He clasped his hands together and breathed out heavily.

"Sam, you need to let go of them. You need to stop drinking." My head began shaking back and forth, and I stood.

"Sam, listen to me," he pleaded. "They're gone—you cannot save them.

Not Sandy, not Tyler, and not Caitlyn either."

"No, you didn't see her. She was there. Her face, it was white as a sheet, and her eyes—her eyes were black, and her lips were a deep red. She was there."

The pastor looked at me. His face was still serious, but it took on a slightly frightened look.

"White skin, you say?"

"Yes, white skin, and she wore a dark, cloak-type dress."

His face went ashen. He was clearly disturbed by what I was saying, so that made two of us.

"And where exactly did you go that she claimed to know about?"

"Where? Uh, well, I went to Pine Beach, the old Admiral Farragut campus, just to look around. I hadn't been there in a while. Then I went over to the Country Cottage Tea Room. I just had a feeling I should go there. And let me tell you, something very weird..." He cut me off.

"Sam," he stood, "I am going to have to ask for your pardon. I have an appointment that I simply must keep."

"What? An appointment?"

"Yes, yes, I must keep it. I'll call you later, and we will continue this conversation." He rose and began to shuffle me out of his office. "I will call you, I promise; I must keep this appointment, it is of utmost urgency. You will have to trust me."

"Of course, Pastor, but..." He was practically shoving me out the door now.

"Goodbye, God bless." And the door shut behind me.

Did God just reject me? I was sure He had not. I am no religious man, by any means, but I know enough to know that God would not turn me away in my time of need. But what had just happened? I walked down the steps into the parking lot to the Chevelle. I could see the pastor in his office through the window. He was on the phone, his back to me. Whomever he was talking to, it was in a very animated manner. Must have been an important appointment.

The Chevelle roared to life; I pushed on the accelerator and the muscle car rumbled its way back to the inn. About to make a left onto Surf Boulevard... and there it was. About two blocks behind me. The black Lincoln. I stopped in the middle of the street with my blinker on. I could have made the left—there was no traffic—but I waited. I waited for that car to get closer. As it pulled up behind me, I threw my door open and stormed out of the car towards the still- moving Lincoln. I stalked toward the car with my finger waving.

"You! Get out of the car!" I yelled like a madman. The car stopped suddenly and I could see the driver, a man, struggling with the column shifter. I reached the driver's-side door and ripped it open.

"Why are you following me?!" I screamed as I reached in and pulled out an old man. He had to be 75 if he was a day.

"Sir, sir, please! I haven't done anything, don't steal my car, don't hurt us, please!" he pleaded with his eyes and his words. I stopped and looked the man over. This wasn't my guy. There was soft crying coming from inside the car. I peered past the man to what must have been his wife, easily 70 as well. She was muttering, "Oh dear, oh dear," and all I could do was stare. I let the man go and mumbled an apology, something about thinking he was someone else, and walked back to my car as if in a daze.

I was clearly losing it and about to take some old man and his poor wife with me. I piloted the Chevelle back to the inn and parked in my usual spot. I walked into the lobby and straight to my office. I wasn't sure who was behind the desk, but Natalie was off, so I didn't really care who it was. I slammed the door and went to the mini-bar to grab another bottle of Jack. It was barely noon and I was going to visit the good doctor.

No. Not today. Not this time. Instead, I picked up my cell phone and dialed Emily's number.

"Sam? Is that you?" she cooed through the phone. I wasn't entirely sure when we had become so familiar with one another, but it felt good, felt natural. I wasn't sure why, but I wanted it to be this way.

"Hey, Emily, just checking to see when you thought you'd be here. I've had kind of a rough couple of days, looking forward to some R&R if you know what I mean."

I swear I could hear her smile and feel her comfort through the phone.

"I can definitely identify with that!" she sang. "And don't you worry,

Sammy, after tonight, neither of us will remember how miserable the rest of the week has been."

Sammy?

"So, when you think you'll be here?"

"I'm on my way now. Should be there by 2 at the latest, and I am so looking forward to spending tonight with you." Did we really hit it off that well? I mean, I know we clicked and were easy with each other when she was here, but isn't she coming on a little strong? Oh hell, who was I to be questioning fate? If it was our destiny to go out, get all wet and naked and never talk again, then so be it. I was okay with that. I needed to be naked with someone, and her perky nipples were calling me through the phone. Still, there was something else here. More than just a physical attraction that I knew we both felt. Some sort of subtext or something I just didn't understand yet. And I was sure I would find out what that was before she left on Sunday.

"Okay, great," I finally responded. "I'll see you then."

"Bye, Sammy," she sang to me.

Again with the Sammy. I've never been a Sammy. Not sure I can ever be a Sammy and I'm quite sure I don't *want* to be a Sammy.

I grabbed my cell and dialed again.

"Hello?" Natalie answered on the first ring. "Sam, what's going on?"

I keep forgetting about Caller ID.

"Nat, can you come over to my office? I need to talk to you about something."

She hesitated and then spoke. "Sam, it's my day off."

"Nat, I know, but this is important. I wouldn't ask if it weren't."

"Okay, I'll be right there. Don't move." I could hear the concern in her voice as the phone went dead. I didn't mean to worry her that much, but I did need her help.

Ten minutes later, I heard a soft knock on my door.

"Sam? Can I come in?" Natalie's soft voice floated through the darkly stained solid oak door.

I walked over to the door and opened it. There stood Natalie in a yellow sundress that brought out the warmth of her chestnut brown eyes and magnified the brilliance of her dark brown hair. She looked like she had just stepped out of a shampoo commercial. The dress hung down just below the knees and made her calves look supple and toned with just the hint of a light tan.

"Sam?"

The dress made her hips seem just ever so slightly wider than her waist, which, in turn, made the hint of cleavage just above it alluring and inviting.

"Sam? Can I come in?" I was staring at her and not hearing her.

"Oh, of course, I'm sorry, Nat." I moved out of the way and watched the dress float across her small, young ass. I couldn't say why at that moment, but I was so attracted to her all she had to do was say yes. I shut the door and stopped, staring at the cold, dark wood for a long minute.

Stop, Sam. You need to drown yourself in something, and that something cannot be Natalie. She is your friend, not your plaything. That was a difficult thing to imagine at the moment. I closed my eyes tightly and turned back to Natalie. She had taken a seat on the couch in my office.

"I assume this is more of a social visit, so I made myself at home on the couch a little bit," Natalie began as she crossed her legs in a motion that most of the time wouldn't even have been noticeable. But as her leg slowly swung up, the sundress rode up her thigh, and I got a good look at her upper thigh that was also toned and just a little tanned. I was lost again.

"So, Sam, what did you want to see me so quickly for? The way you called, the sound of your voice. I have to tell you upfront that I am a little concerned." Her face was earnest and caring. She brushed some hair from her face and tucked it behind her ear while her brown eyes penetrated me.

"Natalie," I began, "I need your help. I'm not going to beat around the bush here with fancy words about what I've been going through and where my mind has been." I was definitely going to leave out where my mind had been in the last five minutes. "You know—you've seen it. Hell, everyone around here has seen it and had to go through much of it with me."

I sat down on the couch next to her.

"I need to stop drinking."

Her eyes brightened, and she reached out and gave me an excited hug.

"Oh, Sam!" She was practically bouncing. "I can't believe you're finally coming around! I knew it yesterday; I could tell. You're ready." She smiled so big and bright, her teeth shone between her soft pink lips. I reached into my pocket and pulled my keys out. She watched me, still smiling, but curious now. I fumbled with the keys, searching for the right one.

"I can't have this key anymore—I don't trust myself with it." I found and removed the key to the liquor cabinet in the pub. I handed it to Natalie.

"Nat, you are now in charge of all the alcohol in the building. Work with

Curtis; make sure the inventory stays stocked. And whatever you do, don't let me have any." I smiled slightly.

She looked at me, holding the key in her hand. Her smile had softened, and I didn't know what to make of the expression on her face.

"Oh," I continued, "and you have full access to my office. You can come in any time to search it for alcohol." Was I going too far with that? Did I really want Natalie coming into my office any time she felt like it? Her face started to crumple a little bit; was she going to cry?

She reached over and hugged me again, this time softly and with warmth.

She held me and didn't let go, so I wrapped my arms around her small waist. I could feel her breathing with what seemed like soft sobs. I began to rub her back gently to soothe her.

"Sam?" her muffled voice came through my shoulder.

"Yes, Nat? It's really not this big of a thing."

"Yes it is. You are healing, and you trust me to help you. And that means the world to me. I'll be here for you." She lifted her tear-stained face from my shoulder, her face only inches from mine. I could feel her hot, wet breath on my cheek. "I always knew the friendship, the relationship we had before, was too strong to let the alcohol destroy it. I prayed for you every night." She continued to breathe huskily into my ear while the words oozed from her lips. "Every night, Sam. I knew God would help you and let me be there for you."

I could feel her firm breasts push up against my chest as she leaned in and gave me the softest kiss on the side of my lips. My arms tightened slightly around her back as I moved my face to return the kiss. Our lips met in a soft exchange of so many things that were never said between us.

Then she pushed me away and stood, her sundress still hiked around mid-thigh.

"Oh, Sam, I am so sorry." She tried to straighten her dress. "I—I—I have to go," she stammered and began to stumble toward the door. "Don't worry,

Sam, you can count on me. I will help you through this." I stood up.

"Natalie..." But she was out the door. I wasn't entirely sure what had just happened here. But I knew that it wasn't over. That was a real kiss, and the warmth in my chest told me I was just as ready for it as she was. I thought about calling her to make sure we were still okay, but I knew we were. I just didn't know exactly where "okay" was right now.

I had showered, put on some jeans, and was just finishing buttoning up a black cotton shirt when my cell rang. It was Emily. She must be here. I checked the time on my phone before I answered—it was almost 3. She was late.

"Hey, Emily, glad you could make it." I said, with layered sarcasm.

"Oh, Sammy, stop it," she blurted out. Sammy again? "Traffic on 195 is

hell and you know it! Come and get me. I'm waiting for you." I found it intriguing how I could feel that sly, sexy smile coming through the phone. She had a way about her, and I didn't know how to deal with it just yet.

"I'll be out in one minute." I snapped my phone shut and bolted out of the cottage. I went through the lobby and found Emily sitting on the trunk of her red BMW 3 series convertible. The top was down, and she looked as sexy as ever.

Her feet hit the ground as she hopped off the trunk, and her blonde hair came undone from where it had been perched on top of her head. It fell over her bare shoulders and in her face. She brushed it out of the way and revealed golden skin on her slim and curvy neck. Her green strapless top covered just enough of her breasts to keep her from getting arrested. I could see her nipples protruding through the thin fabric, which I had no problem with at all. It was a beautiful warm day out, but maybe it was a little colder than I realized. She sported a white pair of shorts that hugged and caressed her near-perfect ass and accentuated her shapely tan legs down to her white sandals and red painted toes. She was a picture, alright, and I couldn't wait to develop it.

She ran over to me, her sandals click-clacking the whole way as she jumped into my arms and gave me a big hug and kiss on the cheek. Again, I was left wondering when we became this familiar. Was it while we were drunk in her room, and I just can't remember?

"Sam! Come on, let's go!" And she was off to the passenger side of her car. "You drive!" And before I could even respond, her tanned butt was firmly in the white leather seat, so I followed and got in the car. I revved the engine, shifted the BMW into first gear, gunned the engine and tore out of the inn's driveway towards the boardwalk.

We drove down route 35 towards Seaside Heights with the wind whipping through the car and tossing Emily's gorgeous blonde hair all over the place. We roared past the

Lake of the Lilies and through Bay Head and still hadn't said anything more to each other. Emily had her head back and her eyes closed throughout the drive. Not until we slowed down around Normandy Beach did

Emily turned her face to me and speak again.

"Miss me?"

I looked at her to see if she was serious—how could I miss her? I barely knew her.

"Of course I missed you." What would you have said?

"No, you didn't, but that's okay. Because you will miss me the next time I go; I'll make sure of that!" she said with a sly smile and slid her hand over my leg to my inner thigh.

"So," I tried to change the subject, "I know you love seafood, so we are going to have the best lobster on the Jersey Shore at the Lobster Shack. It's over on Harbor Island."

She sat up and looked at me.

"Harbor Island? Is that the place you can only get to by boat?"

"That very same one."

"How did you get us a reservation there on such short notice?"

"I didn't, but I know the owner, Jim; he's a great guy. He was a big fan of mine when I was driving."

Emily's eyes widened.

"Driving?" she said in a questioning tone, but I could see her putting it together in her head.

"Driving?" she repeated. "Sam Shepard. You're *that* Sam Shepard?" Her face lit up like the Fourth of July. I just flashed a small smile and nodded my head without taking my eyes off the road. I swung off of West Central

Boulevard onto Bay Boulevard so we could get a view of the bay as we approached the parking area for the restaurant. That felt good. It had been a long time since someone recognized me as a driver. I know—I had to tell her, but still it felt good.

"So here you are, the famous Sam Shepard, and I'm out on a date with you." Emily smiled satisfactorily to herself. I pulled into the parking lot overlooking Barnegat Bay and killed the engine. I looked over at Emily as she unbuckled her seatbelt and watched her breasts bounce as the strap released its support.

"Emily?"

"Sam?" She looked at me expectantly.

"What's going on here? I mean, don't get me wrong. I think you are beautiful and sexy and I'd love to be naked with you, but…" I trailed off.

"But what," she smiled, "am I coming on too strong?" She took my chin in her hand and looked into my eyes.

"Sam, I like you, that's all. You are one hell of a good-looking, single, lonely, successful man, and I am a very lonely woman. We both have demons we need to work through and dreams to explore. Let's do it together, Sam. Neither of us should be lonely." She closed her eyes and sealed that with a soft, lingering kiss. "And the way things are going, you'll get to see my breasts bounce a lot more later tonight." She pulled away with a seductive smile. I supposed I shouldn't look a gift horse—or hottie—in the mouth.

She got out of the car, and I led her down to the dock. The dock master met us as soon as we set foot on the wood planks.

"Good evening, do you have a reservation?"

"No," I replied, "I'm a personal friend of Mr. Farnsworth. Sam Shepard.

Mr. Farnsworth will have a table for us."

"Very good, Mr. and Mrs. Shepard." Emily giggled and blushed at that.

"Please step onto the boat, and I'll radio in that you are on your way."

We stepped over to the water to see a line up of gondolas, each with a gondolier stationed at the stern, pole in hand.

We boarded the closest one, and I looked at the young man.

"Those poles really reach the bottom of the bay out there?" I pointed toward Harbor Island. He laughed at me.

"No, sir. The poles are really just navigation. We have small engines just below where I'm standing. They don't move us very fast, but we get there."

The gondolas were outfitted to take two people across the water to the island the restaurant was on. Emily took the first seat, and I sat in the other. We both had waterside seats, and she leaned into me as the sun began to dip in the sky. The gondolier handed us both glasses of red wine from behind.

"A merlot, compliments of Mr. Farnsworth. He says welcome and looks forward to serving you tonight. He has also asked me to give you the bay tour. It takes about a half an hour and allows some fantastic views of the bay, and we go past the area where you can see directly across the island to the Atlantic."

Emily smiled and looked at me. "That sounds wonderful."

She grabbed my arm, rested her head on my shoulder, and we were off.

We started drinking wine and sailing the Barnegat Bay in a gondola. The wine was sweet and fruity, the views were spectacular, and the company was fantastic. We exchanged some small talk while we enjoyed our trip. I learned that her family was government family all the way through. Her father and brother were in the FBI, and her mother was an assistant on Capitol Hill. Her father was very disappointed that she went into law instead of active FBI service. I filled her in a little about my driving career, the accident, and that I still take painkillers for my back. We arrived at Harbor Island dock at about five and disembarked from our gondola. I helped Emily off the dock to the entrance of the restaurant.

We walked through the door and she stopped, reading the sign.

"Sam." I stopped, too. "This sign says *Lobster Shack Dinner and Breakfast*."

"Yes," I said peering down my nose at the sign, "so it does." I smiled. "Any interest in trying the breakfast?" My smile broadened, and her face flushed. She walked away, shaking her head at me. The hostess, a lovely young brunette in what you might call a "little black dress," showed us to our table overlooking the bay. The restaurant was round and every table had a bayside view. The kitchen was on the floor below, so there were no obstructed views. You could see from one side of the dining room to the other and get a complete 360-degree view of the bay. The sun was just beginning its departure from the sky and was offering up a brilliant orange light show out the west side of the restaurant. It illuminated the entire room and lit up Emily's silky blonde hair like it was on fire. We ordered the house seafood feast, which included lobster, shrimp, scallops, and oysters. We added a bottle of the house merlot we had sampled on the trip over, and we were well on our way to a delicious evening.

We talked, told stories, and laughed for hours. It seemed like it was dark before we knew it, and we were staring at dessert menus after our third bottle of wine. Emily tried to pick up her dessert menu, but her elegant fingers fumbled with it before dropping it back on the table, and she began laughing.

"Methinks the lady is very, very drunk," I offered with a laugh.

Emily continued to laugh, now throwing her head back to an almost cackling sound.

"Would you like me to read the menu to you?" I continued to smile and laugh. Emily stopped laughing and attempted a serious face.

"No," she began with an air of seriousness, "I can do this." Her speech was beginning to slur, and I couldn't keep a straight face but fought the urge to laugh as she fumbled with the menu yet again. This attempt ended in a similar manner to the first: The menu was falling and she was laughing. I finally picked

up the menu, opened it and placed it into her unsteady hands.

"Thank you, SSssssam," she slurred and finished with a giggle. She now had slightly better control of herself. She steadied herself on the table and closed the menu triumphantly.

"I will have," she began with great effort, "the Banananananananazzzzzz

Fosterrrrrr," she slurred heavily now and finished with a giggle.

"Then we will make it two." I smiled and waved the waiter over to place our order. After we placed our order, Emily's cell phone began ringing. She laughed out loud.

"How am I supposed to answer THAT!" She proceeded to fumble through her purse to make the attempt. She frowned when she looked at the Caller ID.

"Stupid director or, I mean, boss, you know," she fumbled for words and seemed to stop short and sober up a little bit. "I mean, never mind."

"Do you mind if I check mine?" I asked, and she consented. I pulled my

iPhone out of my pocket and saw I had two messages. I dialed voicemail and listened. The first message was from Bob, the real estate agent.

"Mr. Shepard, Bob here. Glad you called, and I appreciate the opportunity to earn your business. I did a little bit of research on the property you inquired about. Give me a call when you get a chance, and we can compare notes." He left his number and hung up. Damn, why couldn't he just leave the information on my voicemail? Apparently, he changed his mind because the next voicemail was from Bob again.

"Mr. Shepard, pardon my calling back so soon. I forgot; I am actually heading out of town for a week, so I thought you might like to know that Max Khayman owns the property you inquired about. I will call you when I get back in town. It's not officially for sale, but if you are interested, I would still be able to bring him an offer."

Max Khayman? Is that the same Khayman who owns the Country Cottage Tea Room and the black Lincoln? The threads are coming together, but what are we knitting? I can't see the picture, and Emily is looking at me in a strange way.

"Sam? Everything all right? You look worried." She was still slurring her words, but she was on her way down from her previous high.

"Yeah, yeah, everything is fine. I had called earlier about some real estate, and that was my agent. Just wasn't what I expected, that's all."

"Oh yeah?" She smiled. "You going to buy this island now?" she giggled.

The Bananas Foster appeared, and we dug into the warm, gooey dessert.

"No, not this island. The old military school campus across the river. I went there, thought maybe I'd renovate the place." And that was not entirely untrue. I had thought about it in the years since the school closed, but I really just wanted to know who owned it at this point. And more importantly, I needed to get inside.

Emily had already finished off her dessert; I was impressed at how such a small woman could put away food. And her demeanor had changed. She was very serious, and I noticed wrinkles around her eyes I had not seen before.

"Military school? You mean the old Farragut place? I've heard it's owned by the mob—did you hear that?"

"The mob?" My interest was piqued. I had heard the Khayman clan called many things before, but not the mob. "I don't know about that. But the Khayman family is very wealthy and powerful around here. How do you know about the school?"

She picked up her wine glass and finished it quickly.

"Just an old case we had a few years back when the school closed and I had read about the sale of the land and buildings. Just in passing, really. Do you know any of them? The Khayman family, I mean."

"Me? No," I responded, "I was just interested in the property, not the people." That, however, was a huge lie.

She smiled slyly. "I've heard they're into witchcraft."

"What?" I laughed. "Witchcraft? What is this, a UPN sitcom? I know they own a lot of bars and run some illegal activity, but witchcraft? That's funny."

She downed another glass of wine—she could really put it away. She leaned forward over the table, the tops of her silky smooth breasts pushing up towards me. I couldn't keep my eyes off them.

"I've heard they kill people who don't do what they want or owe them money and stuff," she confided in me as if it were a secret. So, I leaned forward and took in a big eyeful of those perky breasts and responded.

"I've heard they have tails and are vampires!" I laughed, but she didn't.

She sat up in her chair and regarded me seriously again.

"Vampires? What makes you say that?"

"Oh, I was just kidding, you know. You were making them sound like *The Godfather* meets *Charmed* or *Buffy the Vampire Slayer* or something. So I kind of pulled the vampire thing out of my ass."

She laughed it off. "Yeah, Buffy, that's funny... definitely has to be out of your ass." She smiled; the softness returned to her face, and her eyes seemed to get just a little bit greener as I stared into them. Then she changed the subject.

"Did you have any trouble getting me a room for the night?" she asked playfully.

"Actually," I began, very embarrassed, "I did have some trouble, believe it or not. I couldn't get you a room at the inn." Her jaw dropped a little, clearly surprised. "There is a convention or something in town, so I thought we would figure something out. But, now… sitting here, staring into your captivating eyes, I have a great idea." I smiled slyly and poured her some more wine. She grabbed the glass and looked directly into my eyes.

"What kind of idea is it?" she asked just before she lightly licked her red lips and took a sip of the wine.

"I'll be right back." I smiled, got up, and walked through the dining room toward the hostess station.

"Sam!" she almost yelled. "Where are you going?"

I made my way to the hostess station, and the lovely, black-dressed young lady was there.

"Can I help you?"

Five minutes later, I was on my way back to the table to fill her in on what I had planned for her. But as I approached the table, I noticed Emily wasn't there. I stopped just short of the table, noticing her purse was gone, too. I looked around, figuring with a full 360-degree view I had to be able to spot her.

But I didn't see her anywhere. I went down the center stairs to find the waiter.

Among the hustle and bustle of the wait staff running around, I spotted him.

"Hey, did you see my date?"

"Yes, I saw her heading outside to the deck a few minutes ago."

The deck? I didn't look there. You could see the upper deck from the restaurant, but there was a lower deck that actually went out over the water on the east side. I should have thought of that myself. Back in the dining room, I located the French doors that led out to the deck. I opened them and was hit by the warm, salty air immediately. I walked out to the edge of the top deck and in the twilight, I saw Emily on her cell phone, speaking to someone in a heated conversation. I couldn't hear what was being said, but I could hear her raised tone of voice. I found the stairs leading down to the lower deck and began walking down them, trying to be conspicuous so she would notice me. I didn't want to eavesdrop.

"Yes, sir, I understand but... sir, I..." I began to pick up pieces of what she was saying as I got closer. I coughed audibly; she looked over, smiled and held up a finger, asking for a minute to finish her call. I motioned that it was no problem and went to lean against the railing on the other side of the deck while I waited for her.

"Understood, my ship has arrived, I have to go." She closed her cell phone and sauntered over to me with a sexy smile. I turned to lean my back against the railing and returned the smile. She stopped about six inches from me, cocking her hand on her hip.

"So?" she questioned me.

"So? So what?" I played dumb. "You calling your dad to tell him you might be a little late? The sun has almost completely set—it will be dark in a few minutes."

"Yes, it will be," she responded playfully. "And I have nowhere... and no one... to sleep with."

I handed her the keycard for the *Lobster Shack Inn*. Her eyes lit up, and she smiled.

"You think I'm that easy? You feed me, pour some wine down my throat, and I'm just going to sleep with you?"

"Easy there—I never said anything about me staying. You needed a place to stay." Her face froze. It was readily apparent that she had never imagined I would have just gotten her a room. I could see it in her face and her posture as she took about half a step back.

"Oh, Sam, you're right. I'm embarrassed. Of course, this has been a really great time but..."

I reached over, put my arm around her back and pulled her to me.

"Emily, you talk too much." And I kissed her deeply and passionately.

She wrapped her arms around my neck and returned the kiss. Her lips were soft and smooth, and my tongue parted them deftly. I could feel her tongue reciprocating the light touches of my own as it probed her warm, soft mouth. I felt the keycard dig into my back a little as my hand found the small of her back and gave it a soft caress, then a firm tug to pull her hips into my ever-growing need for her. I moved from her mouth to her neck; the soft scent of perfume intoxicated me, pushing me to run my tongue along the valley of her neck to the bottom of her ear and lightly nibble on it. She pushed me away, breathless now.

"Maybe we should use this," she said, waving the keycard at me.

I'm not sure how long it took us to get to our room, but we practically ran the whole way and it still seemed like an eternity. Emily slid the keycard in the door, pushed it open, and had her arms around me in a matter of seconds. I heard her purse fly against the wall and felt her tongue inside my mouth before I could respond. She jumped up and wrapped her legs around me while I wrapped my arms around her with my hands grabbing each side of her tight ass.

I pushed my mouth down toward her neck and she threw her head back, blonde hair flying, and emitted a low moan.

"Oh, yes, Sam, mmm," and she began to undulate her hips into mine.

"I've been waiting for this, oh yes!"

I was fully aroused, and my erection was pushing at my pants. I could feel the warmth of her pushing down on it. She threw her head to the side and started licking my ear fervently as I walked us to the bed. I practically threw her on the bed and stared into her wild face. Her eyes had an animal passion in them, and she quickly pushed herself back up and began unbuckling my belt.

I reached down, pulling her top over her head to reveal two beautiful and tanned breasts bouncing down from the force. Her breasts were so perfectly in proportion to her tight stomach and body, it was no wonder she didn't have a bra on. She yanked my belt off, unbuttoned my pants, and undid my zipper in a matter of seconds. She stopped for what seemed like eternity when she discovered I wasn't wearing underwear and my fully erect penis was staring her right in the face. She looked up at me, her eyes on fire, licked her lips and took my throbbing penis into her hot, moist mouth. I closed my eyes and moaned loudly as she slowly worked up and down my penis. My hands found her smooth shoulders and made their way down to her breasts, only to find her firm nipples ready for my touch. I rubbed her nipples between my fingers and felt her body convulse slightly. She opened her mouth slightly, breaking contact with my now wet penis, and she let a small gasp escape. The heat of her breath on me was pushing me to my limits very quickly. She took the very top of my penis into her mouth again and began stroking the shaft rapidly with her hand. I grabbed the back of her hair and pulled her off.

"Take off your shorts," I practically ordered. Emily quickly pushed herself back on the bed while I tore off my shirt and kicked my pants away. She unbuttoned her shorts and pushed them down to reveal that she too wore no underwear. She was cleanly waxed, and the sight of her completely hairless and naked body made me want to taste her even more. I wasted no time pushing my open lips and tongue inside of her. I licked and swirled around her and tasted her hotness with each thrust of her hips as she urged me to lick her faster and harder.

But then, suddenly, she pushed me over so I was on my back, and before

I knew what was happening she had straddled my chest, her moist heat pressing against my chest. She grabbed my penis and started stroking it before she moved her way to my face and began pressing herself down on my mouth. I responded with my tongue, passionately working her excitement to a fever pitch.

She began moaning and grabbed me harder as she stroked me over and over. I felt like I was about to explode when I felt her legs tense around my head and she leaned a little forward, pushing so hard on my mouth that I couldn't breathe for a long moment. But I didn't care; I kept going and felt her throw her head back again.

"Yes! Sam, OH GOD!" She kept riding my mouth, back and forth and up and down, until her whole body seized and then shuddered in release. She finally pushed herself off me, only to turn around and hover over my penis. She grabbed it with her left hand, steadying herself with her right hand. I put both my hands squarely on her gorgeous ass and guided her down onto my bulging erection. As I entered her, she was hot like scalding syrup on my oversensitive member. It was all I could do to keep from finishing right there.

"Oh, Emilyyyyy," I practically sang as I mixed a moan with the words.

She took me completely in, slowly, and I felt her hips spasm ever so slightly. Then she slowly raised herself up, and I could see the moonlight accentuating the curves of her muscles into the valley of the small of her back.

She put both her hands on her head, held her hair up, and started humming lightly as she went back down on my penis, and then slowly up again. I placed my hands on her hips to guide her and push her along a little faster. She came down again, this time a little faster, and then up with the same speed increase, then down a little faster still and up at the same pace. The intensity of the humming seemed to match the intensity of the sex. As she picked up speed, she turned her head so I could see her mouth open slightly, and she began to moan a little. The moan increased in volume slowly as she moved faster and faster, working my penis. I sat up while she continued riding me up and down, in and out. I grabbed her breasts from behind and massaged them in short circles that kept urging her on and on.

"Come on baby, keep going, oh yes, almost there," I spurred her on and she seemed to respond. Finally, she was moving so quickly her body was slapping against my thighs, and she was moaning and gasping loudly now. I couldn't hold back any longer; the hot friction of her grabbed at my penis and pulled me into the orgasm that had been building since the first time we met. I felt myself completely empty into her as she continued to pump me up and down.

Finally she stopped, and her body spasmed violently again. She had to prop herself up on the bed before finally falling down. We both lay there silently for a long moment, sweat dripping off our hot, drained bodies.

"Emily, that was incredible." I looked over at her smiling face cloaked in her blonde hair as she lay on her stomach. She pushed her hair back and said,

"Yes, that was." We didn't say anything else, just drifted off to sleep with the moon illuminating the room. The last thing I remember seeing was Emily turning over, her still-erect nipples outlined by the soft moon.

It was a pleasant image to fall asleep to, indeed.

March 16th

Unfortunately, when I woke up, the image wasn't as comforting. My eyes fluttered open to an empty bed. I began to lift my head but heard voices coming from the hallway, so I kept my head low. I lifted it slightly and could see the door was slightly open. There were two voices, a man and a woman, and the woman sounded like Emily. I did my best to quiet my breathing and lie still to try and hear what they were saying, but I couldn't quite catch the words. What was she doing and whom was she talking to?

Just as I was about to get up and see, the hallway went quiet, and I heard footsteps retreating from the door. I pushed myself up and sat up on the bed, about to get up when I heard Emily's voice.

"White Dove checking in, sir."

White Dove? What the hell was that? And who was she checking in with?

I quickly lay back down and pretended to be asleep.

"Yes, sir. Yes, subject is still asleep."

Subject? Did I really know who Emily was?

"Hang on, sir. I need to get to a more secure location."

Emily came back in the room, still on the phone, and crossed to the sliding doors leading out to the deck. She stopped for a moment to look at me, making sure I was still asleep, and went out onto the small deck off the room, shutting the door behind her. I couldn't hear her anymore, only the muffled sound of her voice talking in a quiet manner to "sir."

I checked the clock: 1:45. Sounded like work, but who would she be talking to at work at this time? I decided to get up and make my presence known to her. I got up and stretched like I had just woken, but her back was to the room and she didn't see me. So I went into the bathroom, turned on the light and flushed the toilet. She would surely hear that. I waited a minute, and I heard the door to the deck open and close.

"Sam?" she asked with an unsure level to her voice.

I left the bathroom rubbing my eyes. I was a great actor. It was the scratching of my ass that sold the act, though.

"Sam, sorry, did I wake you? I just needed some air." She stood there wearing my black shirt thrown over her like a towel with only one button buttoned near her navel. I could see the valley of her tanned breasts peaking out from the shirt as it hung lazily over them, accentuating the curves in a very seductive way.

It was a very sexy sight to behold. Then I remembered "White Dove," and my fledgling erection quickly went away.

"Hey, no, I just had to hit the head, that's all. Who were you talking to?"

"Talking to…" she began slowly.

"Yeah, I saw you on the phone when I got up. And you are holding your phone. Who is up at this hour? Telling your girlfriends of your monumental conquest?" I flashed a sly smile her way.

She didn't smile back right away. She looked at the phone in her hand, quickly painted a smile on her face, and crossed over to me. She put her hands on my bare chest and kissed me lightly on the lips.

"Wouldn't you like to know? I have to use the bathroom now, too." And she closed the bathroom door. She still had her phone in her hand, which I found odd. I was left wondering whom had I just had sex with. I crossed the room to the table where she had put her purse, presumably when she woke up to get her phone, and I opened it. I put my hand in it and felt something cold, hard and metallic. A gun. I pulled out the small Glock 26 handgun and looked it over quickly. The small 9mm pistol was sleek and gleamed in the moonlight. I glanced at the bathroom; I could hear her running the water in the sink. I put the gun down quietly on the table and continued looking for her wallet. I pulled the small black leather wallet from her purse and opened it. I stared in disbelief.

"Sam, I can explain."

I looked up to see Emily standing in the doorway of the bathroom, the light illuminating her supple figure. I turned her F.B.I. identification towards her.

"You can explain?" I responded flatly. "What's to explain? You work for the F.B.I. and you aren't a lawyer. Or are you? And all that crap about your husband? You used me! And you used my dead wife to lure me in." I glared at her with a questioning look. "Okay, I was wrong, I guess I do need an explanation. Explain to me how someone could be so cold and calculating, playing on my pain like that."

"Sam, it's not what it looks like." She began walking to me with her hands in front of her, trying to keep me calm. I wasn't really upset yet, but I was well on my way.

"It looks like you're an F.B.I. agent, is that not what this is? A lying, whoring F.B.I. agent who drops her skirt as soon as Uncle Sam asks her to." My voice was still very flat, not betraying the emotion I was feeling. But inside, I was about to explode, ready to let her have it full force. Still, I could see my words were hitting her hard, and heck, maybe she had a good reason for lying.

"Well," she stammered, "yes, that is what that is, but I mean I didn't want to lie to you." She shook her head, closed her eyes, and pursed her pretty little lips. "I mean it didn't start out that way. When we met last weekend, what I told you when I was drunk... that was all true. Well, mostly... and I *was* really upset about it. That wasn't all an act."

It? What the hell is *it*? That thought must have registered on my face because the look on hers went to shock.

"Oh," she said simply and looked down. "You don't know what I'm talking about, do you? Dammit! Me and my big mouth!"

"Well, Agent Emily Noble, no, I don't know what you are talking about, but you had damn-skippy better tell me. What do you mean 'mostly?' And now would be a good time, since I am standing here holding your purse." I reached down and picked up the gun. "And your gun. The feds don't take too kindly to agents losing their guns, do they? And I have to be totally honest—the purse doesn't go with my outfit." I stared at her, my eyes like daggers directed right at the lying little slut. I had suspected something about her when I heard the phone call, but now she had confirmed that it wasn't just her job she was lying about.

"Come sit down," she motioned me toward the bed, "and I'll explain. And can I have my gun back, please?" She reached her hand out. I looked at her with disdain and contempt.

"Forgive me if I don't trust you at the moment; I'll stay here and"—I paused for effect—"I'll hang on to this for now." I shook her gun in my hand. "Now, that explanation?"

"Sam." She looked me straight in the face and changed her tone to a serious, professional sound. "I am a special agent as part of the F.B.I.'s Special

Affairs detachment. We are in charge of hunting down and ferreting out special groups that local law enforcement is not equipped to handle."

"Special Affairs?" I responded quizzically. "What kind of special groups can the local authorities not handle? Are we talking mafia or aliens or what?

And what on earth does that have to do with me?"

"Sam, I'm on your side here," she said pleadingly. "Don't make me your enemy."

"You didn't answer my question."

She began speaking, but she clearly wasn't happy with herself for being in this situation.

"I am here in an on going investigation of the Khayman clan. The bureau sent me to try and get information from you about the clan."

"Me? I don't know anything about them. Never met them, never spoken to any of them. At least not that I know of, except that black car that keeps hanging around, but wait—" I put her purse and ID down on the table but kept the gun in my hand and began pacing back and forth.

"That day at the inn, that was a setup. You didn't have any problems with your reservation—you didn't have one. Did you?" She looked a little embarrassed. "And you knew I was roaming the halls that night and would hear you crying. It was all a setup!" My anger was growing inside me as I paced. My arms were flailing, gun in my hand. Emily began to look nervous.

"Sam? Sam, calm down!"

"You!" I pointed the gun at her quickly, like a finger, and she flinched.

"You lying little whore, what was all this tonight?" My arm fell to my side.

"Sam, I swear this wasn't supposed to happen. I—I was just supposed to get to know you, try and get information from you, that was all, but..." She trailed off and looked away out the deck doors. "But I like you, Sam."

"You like me?" I answered, incredulous.

"Yes! I like you, and this—" she pointed to the bed, "—this was real. This was something spectacular. I don't sleep with people—and I certainly don't give blowjobs to get information from people. And you clearly don't know anything about the Khaymans anyway. I knew that before dinner was over. That is what I was doing on the phone, telling my supervisor that you didn't have any useful information."

"What about the man in the hall? Who the hell was that?"

She looked a little surprised.

"The man in the hall? That was another field agent checking to make sure

I was all right. I didn't report in on schedule, which would have been just about the time we passed out." She finished her sentence with a little smile on her lips. For some reason, I now believed her. This was just a job that went too far. I put the gun down on the table, went to the bed, and sat down.

"Well, Special Agent Emily," I sighed, "why are you here? What made the

F.B.I. think I had anything to do with the Khaymans?" Emily came and sat next to me, throwing one of her legs up on the bed and underneath her.

"Sandy," she said simply. "We have intelligence that shows a connection between Sandy and Max Khayman."

"What?" I practically screamed. "What would Sandy have to do with Max

Khayman?"

"The same thing my husband does. We know they knew each other, and we suspect that the Khayman clan had something to do with her and your children's disappearances. I've been following this since my husband disappeared."

"Your husband? How is he involved?"

"I'm not sure, but what I am sure of is that the Khayman clan was responsible for his death. They wired his ignition and blew up his car."

"Wait." I stood up and looked for my pants. "The picture!" I found my pants and pulled out my wallet, opened it and removed the picture I found in the

Lincoln. It was all coming together as I unfolded the picture and saw Sandy laughing, across from a pretty little blonde woman. Emily. How had I missed her there before?

"You were in her book group!" I showed her the picture.

"Yes, but where did you get this?" She looked the picture over.

"At the tea room, the car in the back; it was in the trunk in a suitcase."

"In a suitcase in the trunk of the car in the back of the tea room? What were you doing there, Sam?"

I looked her straight in the eye.

"I heard what you said, you believe it, the F.B.I. believes it. Sandy, Tyler and Caitlyn... they are alive. And I was looking for them. I doubted myself after yesterday, thought it was all a coincidence, too much drinking, but now... with what you have said... I stopped drinking, you know. But it's not a coincidence, is it?" I quickly went over the details about the black Lincoln, the "hallucinations" I was seeing, *Portrait of a Lady,* and how I thought I was losing my mind so I just had to go and look around.

"That's what led me to Farragut and the tea room. I thought they were connected; now I'm 100% certain. Khayman owns the tea room, Farragut, and the car that has been watching me. I still don't know why. Why am I seeing Sandy? Why are they following me?"

And that's when it really hit me. Emily was right. Sandy was mixed up with Khayman, and that's why they were gone.

"Sam, we aren't sure. They may be alive, they may not—there's no way to know. What we do know is that the Khaymans were involved, and that car accident was no accident."

I was still shell-shocked at the revelation. Was Sandy a criminal? Did she have deep ties in the mafia? How would I ever know?

"What now?" I asked. Emily took my hand and looked in my eyes.

"Sam, I don't think we can do this—" she looked down at the bed for a moment and smiled pleasantly, "— again. As wonderful as that was... I need to continue my investigation, and you are a part of that. With what you have just told me, I am more certain than ever that we are on the right track to nailing

Khayman."

"Nailing Khayman?" I said absently. "What about Sandy and the kids?"

"If they are alive, we will find them. If. I think they are all alive, along with my husband. His car blew up, but there was no body, just like Sandy, Tyler and

Caitlyn's accident."

I needed a drink then more than ever. Could they all be alive somewhere? No way.

But they never found any bodies.

"What can you tell me about Natalie Sullivan?"

"Nat?" I answered with a question in my voice. "She's the best person I know. She is honest, doesn't lie or make up stories about dead husbands or anything." Emily looked hurt by that, but screw her. I was still mad at her.

"Nice, Sam. No, seriously. She's very involved in her church?"

"Church? Yes, she is a good Christian woman as far as I know. Goes every Sunday, has Bible study at her apartment. She volunteers whenever she can around the church. I can't believe she would have anything to with this." But I didn't want to believe Sandy did, either. Maybe they were in it together; but then why take Sandy and not Natalie? And what do the kids have to do with it? Were they nothing more than unfortunate victims of circumstance? I suppose I looked at them that way before, anyway.

"Natalie isn't a suspect, just a person of interest. Like you are, Sam. We don't think she is involved, but we feel she knows something about what is going on. She might have vital information."

"Emily, I want to go home." I stood up and put on my pants. "Can I have my shirt back?" She looked at me a little sheepishly, as if she didn't want to take it off in front of me.

"Seriously? That is one of the nicest pair of breasts I have ever had the pleasure of having in my mouth. Don't be shy, take the shirt off, I've already seen them... touched them... licked them..."

She reached over and smacked my arm.

"That's enough, jerk." She unbuttoned my shirt quickly and handed it to me, one arm covering her breasts. I took the shirt and whistled at her as she grabbed her shorts and pulled them on, her breasts bouncing pleasantly along.

I'm gonna miss them. I was a little less mad now.

On the drive back to the inn up Route 35, we didn't say anything to each other. Just watched the ocean-side scenery blow by at 45 miles per hour. We kept the top down—it was a warm night, and I needed the air. We got back to the inn at 3:30, and I gave Emily the keys to the cottage.

"You go stay in the cottage. I'm going to sleep in my office tonight."

"Sam, that's not necessary. I can sleep on your couch; you can have your own bed."

"Agent Emily, I really just want to be alone now, good night." And I walked away, leaving her standing in the parking lot with the keys in her hand.

The lobby was empty, no one behind the counter. It wasn't unusual for the counter person to walk around at night and check the place out, so I wasn't alarmed or annoyed. What I needed now was a drink. I opened my office door and let it slam behind me as I threw my keys onto the side table by the couch. I walked over to the mini-bar and opened the door. I grabbed my usual glass, reached for Jack, but he wasn't there. Where was he? Was I out? Then it came back to me: "Natalie," I exclaimed out loud.

"Yes, Sam?" her voice came quietly from behind my desk.

"Natalie!" Shock and surprise were apparent in my voice as I turned to face my desk. My desk chair spun around to reveal Natalie, her dark hair hanging over her shoulders. She sat and stared at me for a minute before standing, leaning both her arms on the desk, revealing her loose-fitting white cotton blouse that hung forward just enough so I could see she was not wearing a bra.

"Sam, what are you doing? You asked me to make sure you didn't drink, and that is what I am doing. I cleared out all the Jack Daniels and cleaned up in here a little while I was at it."

"Nat, I know; I just forgot for a while. It's been a long night, and I needed... something."

She stood straight up and rounded the desk to reveal her smooth-skinned legs, only partially hidden by a short green skirt that was loose fitting but nowhere near knee-length. She usually did not dress so provocatively, but tonight she was smoking hot. She let her hair hang down so that it pressed down ever so slightly on her blouse, bringing out the small yet firm curves of her breasts. I hadn't turned on the office light when I came in, but the light from the courtyard outside silhouetted her firm stomach and the bottom curves of her breasts and nipples as she came around to face me.

"I'm not going to let you indulge yourself. Not physically or spiritually."

Her face was serious, yet soft and caring. "I'm here for you, Sam." She put her hand on my arm and looked into my eyes.

"I know you are, Nat, and I appreciate it. I just wanted to be alone—that's why I came here instead of going to the cottage. Emily is sleeping in the cottage tonight."

Her expression changed to confusion.

"Emily? Noble? In the cottage?"

"Yeah." I broke her hold and dropped myself heavily on the couch. "Can you keep a secret?" Natalie looked at me with a crooked smile.

"Of course I can; what you got for me? She's really a guy? I knew it! Her body was way too perfect." She laughed a little too loud and covered her mouth to stifle the sound.

"No," I said with a small smile on my face. I really wasn't in the mood to laugh. "Emily is actually an F.B.I. agent, and she is investigating Sandy's death."

Natalie's face went blank.

"F.B.I? But why would the F.B.I. investigate Sandy's death? It was obviously an accident." She said it, but not in a way that made me believe *she* believed it.

"They think the Khayman clan had something to do with the 'accident.' I don't know," I continued, a little exasperated, "it seems so far-fetched and such a crazy idea, but they think that Sandy was mixed up with Khayman somehow."

"Wow," she said, but didn't really sound surprised, "Sandy with the

Khaymans? I can't imagine."

"I know, it's crazy, but things have been so weird around here lately with the Lincoln hanging around..."

"Yeah, and the picture from yesterday." She stopped and covered her mouth.

"Picture?" I said suspiciously. "I didn't tell you about the picture—how did you know about that?" My eyes bore into her, searching for an answer from this woman I trusted implicitly, but who clearly wasn't telling me something.

"Natalie? I need you to tell me how you knew I found the picture. I know I didn't tell you about it." She evaded my eyes, turned her face downward, and took a deep breath.

"I followed you," she started so quietly I had to struggle to hear her, "to the tea room, the school, the river. I'm sorry, Sam, I was worried; I have been so worried about you." She put her hand on my shoulder and looked into my face.

"Sam, I care about you whether you care about yourself or not, and look, you are starting on the road to recovery now by kicking drinking."

I looked at her, hard. I didn't believe her.

"How did you know about the picture? Even if you followed me, you wouldn't have known anything about the picture except that I had one."

"I just assumed... the way you looked at it." Her voice trailed off. She was still lying.

"Natalie, if you are going to shovel shit in my mouth, then you are going to have to go. If I can't trust you, who can I trust?" I stood up, walked to the window, and looked out over the courtyard with my hands on my hips.

"I took the picture," she said softly. I didn't move.

"What?"

"I took the picture, Sam. I was trying to document what was going on, I took a lot of pictures. I don't know how they got it, but from where I'd parked, I could see enough of the picture to recognize it. I took it." I whirled around on her angrily.

"Why, Natalie, why did you take the picture?"

"I know who Emily is; I've known all along." She stopped talking and just looked at me. I was about to prompt her to continue when she said, "I know

Emily from a self-defense class she taught; I took it about five years ago. One day I drove with Sandy to the tea room. She had her normal book club and I just wanted to sit and read, drink some tea and relax, really. When I saw Emily, I mentioned to Sandy that I knew her, and she asked how I know Erica. I asked her if she was sure about the name and she said she was, so I assumed that

Emily was lying to her for some reason. I didn't say anything to Sandy about it, but every week when Sandy had her book club, I followed her. I watched Emily and everything that happened. One day during the book club, I noticed that

Emily kept fiddling with her blouse. She lifted it up slightly, and I saw what looked a lot like a wire. So, I thought she must have been working on something official. So I took some pictures, kept notes, thinking I might need them someday and... To be honest," she laughed at herself, "I'm a little nosy. It's a sin, I know, but I can't help myself sometimes." She got up and stood next to me at the window. She put her hand on my back. "Sam, I care about you. And I cared about Sandy and the children, too."

"But Nat, why? Why did you follow her? Why did you follow me? Don't get me wrong, I'm glad you care, but..." I stumbled to find the right words, "what were you going to do about it?"

"Get help," she stated plainly and unflinchingly. "Sam, I know you look at me and see a weak woman who is smarter than she is tough, but you underestimate me. When I saw Emily come in here to stay, I was immediately suspicious, but then I saw she used her real name, so I let it go. I thought that if she was here on an official investigation, she would have used a fake name or identified herself as F.B.I. right away. But then I saw the two of you together, and I just knew that it couldn't be a coincidence. So I knew I needed to keep tabs on you. Think of me kind of like an amateur detective." She smiled playfully, trying to get me to see the lighter side of this, I'm sure.

"So, what, like Harriet the Spy, only older and—" I looked her over and smiled, "—much hotter?" She blushed and crossed her arms awkwardly over her chest. I knew there was still something she wasn't telling me; I just didn't know how to get it out of her. So, I tried the caring, sensitive man angle.

"Natalie, I'm not helpless. I came to you for help because you are the most honest and trustworthy person I have ever met." I looked away from her.

"More than Sandy, as it turns out. I still don't understand why you would put yourself in the middle of an F.B.I. investigation and not say anything to me about any of it. Especially when Emily showed up here."

"Sam," she began, looking me in the eyes so I could see she was being completely earnest and truthful with me, "it is what God led me to do. I did what I felt was right."

After hearing that, I took her in my arms and then I knew I had made a mistake being physical with Emily. I never really cared for Emily—I just needed a sexual release. The sex was good and physically fulfilling, but it wasn't what I really wanted or needed. It was Natalie I cared for, and she cared for me—I could feel it when she touched me, could see it in her gaze.

We sat on the couch; her head nestled on my shoulder. I knew I had to keep trying to find out what was going on, why the F.B.I. was really here and what really happened to my family. And I felt that Natalie could help. But I couldn't do anything before dawn. I decided to take her at her word, and we both fell asleep.

Time is running out, Sam. You must hurry. You must find them. Come back; they are here and still alive.

I awoke and jumped off the couch so quickly that Natalie went flying onto the floor.

"Sam!" she screamed as she hit the carpet. I looked down and saw

Natalie splayed out on the floor pushing herself up onto her elbows. It was a good position from my perspective, but I wasn't sure that she shared that opinion.

"Oh, God, Nat, I'm so sorry." I grabbed her by the shoulders and helped her up.

"Wow," she said, "no more sleeping together. God must be watching."

She laughed easily. But I wasn't sure God had anything to do with what just happened. The voice was loud and clear in my mind. Sandy was talking to me. But how? She's dead; even she says she can't be saved, so how is she talking to me?

"You okay, Sam? You look like you saw a ghost." Natalie regarded me cautiously. "You don't look very good; you are pale. Sit back down." Natalie guided me back onto the couch.

"Nat, I'm hearing things; I'm seeing things. Either they are still alive and

Sandy is talking to me, or I am losing my mind. What little of it I have left, anyway."

Natalie's expression didn't get any brighter.

"Sandy is talking to you?" she asked with concern in her voice. I couldn't help but offer a wry laugh.

"That's an understatement." I rubbed my face in my hands. "I have seen her, right in front of me, as plain as day. Or night, as the case may be. I hear her in my head; she leaves me notes." I got up and went to my desk and opened the drawer I'd put *Portrait of a Lady* in. "Here, look." I handed her the book, open to the page that had the note stuck in it. "That's Sandy's handwriting in her favorite book. I woke up and it was sitting in front of me on my desk. It wasn't there when I fell asleep, or, well, I mean passed out."

Natalie looked at me with concern and was quiet. I stared at her, waiting for her response, something, anything. I felt like I was going crazy, but at the same time, I was sure I wasn't imagining this.

"Nat, don't just sit there quietly, say something. I know it sounds crazy, and I feel crazy. Hell, that's why I stopped drinking Jack—I thought it was the alcohol. But I know I'm not going insane; this feels so real even though it's surreal!"

"It's not the alcohol," she said quietly. I looked at her and crossed my arms.

"I don't think it is either anymore, but I still don't understand." I ran my hands through my hair. "I have to go back." I said simply.

"Back?"

"Yeah, to Farragut. I have to go back and see what's going on there.

Everything is leading me back to Pine Beach, so I have to check it out. I can't just forget about it."

"Sam," Natalie began carefully, "I believe you. It's real, or, I mean, I think what you are seeing and going through is real," she quickly corrected herself.

She spoke as if she was sure, which both made me feel better and worse at the same time. "But I really want you to think about what you are saying and doing.

Did it ever occur to you that maybe this is over our heads?"

"I might be in over my head; I don't really know. I've been dealing with so many conflicting feelings and experiences over the past couple of weeks; I feel torn in different directions. It's a very frustrating feeling. I feel powerless to make a real decision because I don't know exactly what to believe."

"Okay, I'm leaving now." Natalie got up, gave me a quick hug, and started for the door.

"You are leaving? That's it?" I replied incredulously.

"Yeah, I need to get a shower and get changed and run some errands before my shift at the front desk." Oh, yeah, she works here. Slipped my mind.

But it still seemed like she was bidding a hasty retreat for some reason.

And with that, she walked out the door and was gone. I was still unsure of what was going on and didn't feel any better about the situation.

I tried to drown myself in some paperwork for the inn, paying some bills and checking payroll, but it wasn't working. I had so much running through my head. The scene at the church with Pastor Paul, Emily being an F.B.I. agent, some sort of budding romance with Natalie, and last but not least, my hallucinations. Real or not, that's what I'm going to call them. Hallucinations.

The sun was up and the morning was getting late, so I thought I'd head over to the cottage and see what Emily was up to. I would have expected to see her by now. I walked into the cottage to find nothing but silence.

"Emily?" I walked through the living room to the bedroom. It didn't even look like she had slept here. Did she just ditch me last night? I guess it's not really a big deal in the end, but I was a little surprised.

I turned to leave and saw a hairbrush on the sink in the bathroom— Emily's hairbrush. So she had just left quickly this morning without saying goodbye. Again, not a big deal, just a surprise. I went to the door, shut it and went to put my key in to lock it and saw the blood. On the door just below the handle. I hadn't seen it before—I wasn't looking at the handle when I came in— but there was clearly a pentagram was drawn in blood on the door. Something was wrong, very wrong.

I ran back to my office and called Becky. I explained that Emily stayed in the cottage last night but was gone now and there was blood on the door.

"Sam, it's probably nothing."

"Becky, it's something. I can feel it. You have to trust me on this. At least come by and take a sample, try and match the blood. For goodness sake, it is in the shape of a pentagram! That proves it wasn't just someone cutting their finger on the door handle. Someone did it purposely for me to find!"

"But even if it is hers, why would a lawyer be in our DNA database?"

"She's not a lawyer." I said plainly, "She's F.B.I."

That got Becky moving. She showed up with two black and whites ten minutes later. They gave the cottage a thorough once over, collecting hair samples and scraping a blood sample off the door.

"If that is her blood, we will know later today," she began, "but I have to warn you. If it is Emily Noble's blood, the F.B.I. is going to be here faster than you can say 'I've got a boo-boo.' And I'm going to tell you this one more time:

Stay out of this. Stay home, watch SportsCenter. Whatever is going on here is something you can't handle on your own. That pentagram is serious business, got it?" The depth in her dark eyes told me she was serious about this.

I looked hard at Becky. "You've seen this before, haven't you?"

She pushed her dark hair over her shoulder and returned my look. Then she carefully responded, "Yes, at a couple of crime scenes." She began speaking slowly, then picked up pace to try and be reassuring, but it didn't really work. "But usually, there's a body inside. Not this time, which proves that the situation is different. We'll take it from here. Stay home, got it?"

"Yeah, I got it." I thanked her for her help and walked back toward the lobby. The police could handle it from here. Right? This weekend kept getting weirder and weirder.

It was past noon already, and I hadn't eaten anything. I thought I would pop in the lobby and see if Natalie wanted to get something to eat. But when I got to the front desk, Natalie was not there—Stephanie was. Stephanie was supposed to be there, but so was Natalie. Stephanie told me that Natalie said she had something important to take care of and would be back soon.

I shook my head in disappointment and bewilderment and then went over to the pub to grab something to eat. It was surprisingly quiet for midday. Only three tables sitting, and no one at the bar. I couldn't see Curtis but could hear him rustling around in the back for something. As soon as I sat down, Curtis came over.

"Hey boss, we're almost out of Grey Goose. You think you could order some up?"

"Sure, let me write it down before I forget." I fumbled for my iPhone to write the note down but realized I left it in my office when I was with Natalie.

"Hey, can you get me a BLT? I'll be right back—I left my phone in my office." I left the pub and crossed the lobby, noticing Natalie was still not back. I got to my office and opened the door. When I walked in, there was Natalie with Pastor Paul sitting on my couch, as if they were waiting for me. I had the sinking feeling that just when I thought my weekend couldn't get any worse, it was about to go south very quickly.

"Pastor? Nat? What's going on? This feels eerily like an intervention or something." Before they could respond, Curtis came in the door behind me, shutting it behind him. Natalie came to me and hugged me tightly. She had changed into a light blue button-down shirt and loose-fitting denim skirt with sandals. At least she had actually gone home like she said. Not everything was a lie.

"It is, in a way," began Curtis, "but I think Pastor Paul should be the one to explain why we are here like this." I turned away from Curtis to Pastor Paul.

"Pastor?"

He got up and crossed the room to stand right in front of me. Natalie retreated back behind my desk,

"Sam, do you know what the *Pius Sacratus* are?"

I stared at him blankly and was pretty sure my look said it all.

"I'll take that as a no; how about *Comitissa Nocturnus*?"

My expression started to turn towards exasperation.

"Pastor, let's just say I didn't do very well in high school Latin. You wanna do some translating for me?"

Natalie spoke this time from behind my desk. "Sam, do you remember a few months ago when I started inviting you to my Bible study group?" I nodded at her. "Well, it isn't exactly a Bible study group." Curtis came around and sat on the couch in his usual rough blue jeans and untucked black button-down shirt.

Natalie's pause was a little too long for my liking, so I spoke up.

"Well, what was it... what is it? And what does Curtis have to do with it all? I've never seen Curtis at church a day in my life."

At that, Curtis gave a snort. "That might be true, my friend, but I am a very religious man. Back when you had your accident and were still in traction in the hospital, I sought out help to pray for you and your family. I found Pastor Paul, and he immediately saw something in me that took my breath away."

"That's right, Sam, and since Sandy and the children were taken, I have seen it in you, too. But we are getting a little ahead of ourselves. To begin, we are the *Pius Sacratus*—it translates from Latin as Holy Warrior. I was chosen, as were Natalie and Curtis. There are hundreds of *Pius Sacratus* around the world, doing battle to ensure that

God's Will is done on Earth. I know, I know—" he waved his hands in the air as he whirled around, "—it sounds like a big, vague job." He spun and pointed his finger at me. "But it isn't! In fact, the *Pius*

Sacratus are charged with a very specific job, and the mark of the *Sacratus* is on you, too." I turned away from him for a moment, noting that no one had really answered my question.

"Mark?" I replied while turning back to them.

"On your soul, Sam. I saw it on you that night in the cemetery. Even with all the liquor in you, it was bright as a lighthouse."

"And, not to sound repetitive, what is it that this *Pius Sacratus* does, exactly?" I made sure to emphasize the 'exactly' part. "And what about that other Latin thing you asked about?"

"It really begins with the *Caelitus Nocturnus.* Translation, Lord of the Night, or Night Ruler. The *Caelitus Nocturnus* is a very widespread species of demons that only appear at night and take their new members as payment for mortal world debt without asking and without permission. They feed on mortals... God's people, on their flesh and blood and many times, people don't even know it. They wake up in the morning and feel sick or tired, notice what looks like a bug bite on them and wonder where they got it."

"Sounds like you're vampire hunters to me," I said plainly, "and I don't really believe in vampires."

"Well," began Pastor Paul, "in a way, we are. The *Caelitus Nocturnus* are vampires of sorts, but there are many different types of vampires in the world, from those who simply hunt and eat to those who control industry and mingle among humans like any other. The latter is what we have here. The *Caelitus Nocturnus* are capable of being out and about at any time. They are stronger than other types of vampires—the sun does not kill them; it simply drains their energy and dries them out. So they can only be out in the daylight for short periods of time. This makes them increasingly powerful and dangerous."

"And how can you not believe in vampires? Even after the pentagram on your door?" Natalie chimed in. "That's their sign; they marked you, but you weren't there. You were with me—they probably took Emily instead, and we have to save her."

"Save her?" I replied incredulously. "How in the world are we... are you going to save her? We don't know who took her or where they went."

Curtis looked up from the coffee table. "Yes, boss man, we do. They came for you just like they came for Sandy." My jaw dropped, and I almost fell over. I had to brace myself against the bookshelf.

"Sandy?"

"Yes," began Pastor Paul, "when you came and told me what you were seeing and experiencing, it sounded like *Caelitus* activity to me, so I called my superior and told him what was going on. Natalie came to me this morning with your most recent sighting of Sandy and the truth of it is, Sandy is a *Comtissa Nocturnus,* or at least it sounds like it. She would be one of the senior female members in the clan, appearing like a dream but being very real, moving quickly, only visiting at night, leaving messages... it's all there. And if she is trying to tell you that Tyler and Caitlyn are still alive, then they are. That means have to save them, too!"

"Sam," Curtis added, "the *Caelitus* only take those who owe them or have been bound to them. Sandy must have owed them in some way, but when they came for her, Tyler and Caitlyn must have been in the way and got caught up in the middle of it. They won't kill children—often they keep them until they reach adulthood and then make them part of the clan."

"So, they *are* still alive?" I was truly hopeful for the first time in a very long time. "We have to go get them! But what about Emily? And why would they come for me?"

The pastor responded to that, "Emily will either be turned into a sex slave for the master of the clan or killed outright. But nothing will happen to her until midnight. My guess is that you were getting too close to them or that they fear

you in some way, so they came for you. Natalie said you spent the night with her last night"—Natalie visibly blushed and looked away—"so they found Emily instead and took her. It could very well be a ploy to lure you into a trap. They may be assuming you will come after her."

"Damn straight! I'm gonna kick some ass and get my family back!"

"We don't think they know that you know what's going on," began Natalie.

"It looks like they expect you to wander around looking for Emily, and they might have a trap waiting. Except now, you have us with you. And they won't expect you to be looking for Tyler and Caitlyn, either."

"Not for nothing and no offense, Nat, but I wouldn't think you'd be much of a fighter, and this is probably pretty dangerous."

They all laughed out loud, and Curtis fielded that one.

"Sam," he slapped my back, "Natalie could take all three of us very easily.

She is a black belt and world-class gymnast, among other things. I handle explosives and firepower, and Pastor

Paul—well, he can hold his own, and he is the holy man, after all."

"Okay, so let me sum this up for everyone. What we have here is a band of super vampires who can be out in the sunlight, and they're not only very strong, but they also control industry? What kind of industry?"

"Boardwalks, casinos, restaurants, strip clubs—it's mostly organized crime type stuff," Curtis said matter-of-factly.

It hit me like a brick. "Khayman!"

"Exactly," said the pastor, "we can't prove any of this to anyone, but we know the Khayman clan, with Max at the head, has been at this for over one hundred years and is getting stronger. They are showing their strength, first by taking Sandy and now, Emily. They seem to come and go as they please."

"So you say I have this mark on me. What do I bring to the party?"

With that, Natalie looked at Pastor Paul and Curtis glanced at him, too.

Pastor Paul smiled.

"Sam, my superiors and I think you are the chosen one: The vampire hunter we have been waiting for who, as it has been foretold, will come and cleanse the world of the *Caelitus Nocturnus* curse forever."

It took everything in me to keep from laughing out loud.

"Are you serious? Me? A vampire hunter? I don't think that would be a really great idea."

"No, no, you misunderstand me, Sam. You have been chosen by God.

It's not a matter of being a good idea or you liking it. It is your destiny. It is who you are, it is your calling. It is why you went to Pine Beach in the first place. You knew they were there; you just didn't know how you knew. I am telling you now how you know all of this. It is within you. And you aren't simply a vampire hunter; you are *Pius Sacratus.*"

I was dumbfounded—it was all so much to take in, and I wasn't sure how much I believed, anyway. Yet as I looked from face to face, from Curtis to Paul to Natalie, I found myself believing it more and more. These were the three people in the world I trusted the most. And they all believed my children were still alive.

"You really think Tyler and Caitlyn are there? Alive?"

They all nodded to me.

"Then what in blazes are we doing standing here talking—let's go get them. Let's go get all of them!"

With that, the gang all came together and hugged.

"Sam," Pastor Paul began, "I need you to understand, with what you have

told us about Sandy, she cannot be saved. She is one of them."

Deep down, I already knew that, but it still hurt when he reminded me. All

I could do was nod my head.

"Okay," Paul began, "first we pray. Dear Lord, please give us the strength and wisdom to carry out Your will first and foremost. We pray that You would protect and keep safe Tyler, Caitlyn and Emily and that You would be there with us on our quest to free them from their evil captors. Amen." We all repeated the end of the prayer.

"Let's all meet at the sanctuary in an hour. We will form our plan and go over the gear with Sam. We are going to get them, and we are going tonight!"

Everyone agreed and began to exit through my office door. Natalie stopped for a moment and looked back at me.

"You know all those vacations I took? The two days here and three days there?"

"Yeah," I answered.

"This is what I was doing."

She walked out. And I enjoyed watching her small frame walk out the door and through the lobby. I wonder if she dressed up for these sorts of things?

That would be interesting.

I was seriously conflicted about this whole situation. If all of this was true, how could I have enough faith in God to see me through this, after everything God put me through? How much does one man have to lose? I think my biggest fear isn't that they *are* right and I *am* this über-vampire hunter. Because I am going to get my children back and if they are right I'm going to kick their asses. But what if they are wrong, and I'm not? We go to the school tonight and nothing's there? It would just prove to me that my pessimism toward religion has a strong foundation. That everything done in God's name is a joke. At this point I think that would kill me. I don't think I can believe in this and be let down. I just can't be let down again. I went over to my desk to fire up iTunes again. Decided a little Katie Melua was what I needed to mellow me out, and help me gather my thoughts before the big meeting this afternoon. Nothing was ever going to be the same.

But that's a good thing, isn't it? Things aren't so rosy now.

Funny thing—while I sat behind my desk listening to Katie belt out *I wonder if love will pass me by/ Now that I found you, I'll call off the search,* I realized I wasn't hungry anymore.

March 16th, 3:00PM

After I killed the rumbling engine of the Chevelle, I sat in the church parking lot for a good five minutes. Curtis' pickup truck was there, as was Natalie's sea-foam green Cavalier convertible. The only thing that saved the car was the white ragtop—that sea-foam shade was truly horrible. But there I was, sitting and stalling, kvetching about the color of a car. Part of me was so pumped up to get there and do this, and another part of me was too afraid of what could happen here.

I walked into Pastor Paul's office and found my three friends standing over a table, going over what looked like a building layout. But holy crap—pardon my French—Natalie had on a skintight two-piece lycra bodysuit that left very little-to- nothing to the imagination. It was black and hugged her hips like water rolling down her silky skin. Her hair was pulled back, and she looked stunning. Curtis had on what looked to be old military fatigues and a flack jacket loaded up with various explosives. Pastor Paul was dressed a little more sensibly, but still in all black.

With his long black overcoat, he looked ready for action. I suddenly felt very underdressed in jeans and a tee shirt.

Natalie was the first to notice me come in. She shot me a soft smile and mouthed a quick "Hi," and I waved back. Curtis lifted his head and shook it quickly.

"Sam, Sam, Sam… what are we going to do with you? Look at this! You look like you're going clubbing. Did you actually do your hair for this?" He laughed out loud. "Here, put this on." And he threw me what appeared to be a black Special Forces vest.

"We really don't care what you wear, but you need to be prepared. Natalie likes the whole Mission Impossible look, and for her, a good look it is," he added with a wink. "But that vest is all you really need."

It was very heavy, Kevlar-lined, and snapped on comfortably. I felt around the pockets and found a Glock 26, just like the one Emily had, in one pocket.

Several magazines, with what looked like silver bullets, were in another, and in the inner pocket (and seriously adding to the weight) were a half-dozen 6-inch silver stakes. I felt the other inner pocket and pulled out an 8-inch silver crucifix with a sharpened point at the end. Wherever I was going, whatever I was going to face, I was well prepared!

"Sam, my boy," the pastor began, "I think it's time we filled you in a little... debunk some vampire myths and tell you the real story about how all this works."

"Pastor," I began, "I want to know everything I need to get my children back."

"Then let's start here, with some of the common myths. Holy water?

Out—it only makes everyone all wet. Crucifix? Does nothing but irritate them."

"But what about this?" I interrupted, pulling out what I mentally called the Christ- stake.

"Oh, that—well, see, it's in the form of the crucifix more for function then anything else. Take a hold of it, go ahead."

As I grasped the one side of the crucifix, the long top sat nicely on my forearm, allowing me to control the sharp end quite easily.

"So, it's like a heavy dagger?"

"Well, yes and no. There are only three ways to kill a *Caelitus*. The first is loads and loads of sunlight. Yes, they can get around in the daytime, but let's say one fell asleep at the beach. He would whither up in a couple of hours. Not a practical way to kill them, really."

"Unless you want to torture the hell out of them!" chimed in Curtis with maybe a little too much enthusiasm.

"Nice," offered Natalie, "we've done it once or twice, Sam, but not as punishment. It just worked out that way when we were on a mission in Egypt."

"Egypt?" I gasped a little.

"Yeah, we go all over," Natalie said while she checked her pack one last time. I didn't see what was in it, but she seemed pleased with it.

"It's all part of the job," Pastor Paul continued. "The second—and very popular with Curtis—method is beheading. A nice clean cut, and the *Caelitus* in question is surely a goner. Now, they don't die right away. The head can survive without the body, so be careful. If you want to ensure a kill, you have to shove a silver stake or dagger in the evildoer. The silver is what poisons them, and even a small amount, if ingested, will eventually kill them. But nothing is quite as effective as ramming the silver crucifix through one of them. They die within seconds."

I put the Christ-stake back in its holder and took out the Glock.

"What about this?"

"Oh, that," Paul answered, "That has silver bullets in it. I know, I know, sounds cliché, but it works. If you run out of silver bullets, you can use normal sounds. However, they won't kill the beasts, only stun or wound them. They heal rather quickly, as you will find the first time you ram a shovel in the belly of one, only to watch him remove it himself."

"Nice," I said quietly, "this sounds like it is going to be loads of fun." I looked down at my hands. Was I ready for this?

"Well, Sam, I have to tell you," began Curtis, as if he were reading my mind, "I don't think I've ever seen anyone who is as ready for something like this as you are. And our goal here is to avoid the *Caelitus* tonight. We don't want conflict—we want to find Tyler, Caitlyn and Emily and get them out." Curtis stopped and looked around the room. Natalie stepped up and spoke next.

"That's right, gentlemen," she said with a deep sense of urgency. "Those children have been in hell far too long. This is a rescue mission."

And so it was. We continued to go over the weapons we had and how we could best use them if we had to. Then we went back over to the table to go over the plans for our invasion of the vampire nest.

"There are many entrances to the building," I said. "How are we going to choose the right one, and how are we going to cover the others?"

"It's not about covering them, necessarily," began Curtis, "but we want to make sure they can't grab the kids and get out without us knowing it. That's why we are going to enter here"—he pointed at the map—"the old entrance to the tailor shop. Remember it, Sam?"

"Of course—the hallway goes down about ten feet to a door. It used to be an old wooden door, but I don't know what they've done with it now."

"My sources tell me it still looks like the same wooden door, but it is reinforced with steel for strength."

"Sources?" I looked at Curtis questioningly.

"Don't worry about it, Sammy." He smiled. "The rest of the doors will be loaded up with C4 explosives and remotely detonated to seal them off. My count has fifteen possible exits total, including all of the floors. That's not including the exit to the roof. I'm not sure how I could secure that other than blowing out the fire stairs, which we are doing."

"Excellent," continued Paul, "and our timing couldn't be better. Most of the minions won't be at Farragut Hall because it will be nighttime and they will be out feeding. But Max Khayman is known for staying in on Sundays since his strip clubs are closed. And the only thing he really enjoys is the evil lure of the naked woman. He does not need to leave the clan to feed—the innocents are brought to him. As Curtis said, we're not looking for a fight, but at the same time, we want to shut this den of inequity down once and for all, if we can, by blowing it to kingdom come!"

"Once inside," Natalie continued, "we will follow the main corridor down to the lower levels of the building. We will split into two teams there. Unfortunately, we don't have any maps of the sub-basement areas of the building. The building itself was constructed in the late 1800s, and who knows what they put underneath it back when it was a brothel and hotel. Remember, the goal is to locate the children and, if possible, Emily, and get them out. We are closing all known exits off only after we locate the children. We don't want to alarm anyone who might be down there before we have to. And there is a good chance that we won't be able to communicate with each other, so both teams will carry a detonator for the explosives. When you find the kids, blow the place sky high. If you hear the bombs going off, head back to the tailor's door immediately. Who knows how long the old place will hold up under all that shaking? And, with any luck, we will trap Max Khayman and his clan in a fiery death."

"Including Sandy," I added with sadness rich in my tone.

"Sam," Natalie began to walk over to me, "we can't save her. She is already one of them. She told you herself."

"I know, I know," I repeated almost to myself. "I just feel... I don't know what I feel. I've let go of her. I did a while back. But I never let go of the emptiness, and now it's not empty. I have this"—I pointed to the map—"I have you guys and, maybe, if it's God's will, I will have my children back." Natalie wrapped her arms around me in a big hug that was quickly followed by Curtis and Pastor Paul. Still stuck in a group embrace, Pastor Paul said, "It's time to go. Let's all bow our heads in a word of prayer."

"Right on!" chimed in Curtis. And we all grasped one another's hands in a circle. Together, as a team, we formed an unbreakable circle of strength, a circle of support, a circle of faith. Together, we were one. Then Pastor Paul began praying.

"All-merciful and knowing God, we beseech You to be with us on this, our first mission together. A mission of mercy to free Tyler, Caitlyn and Emily from the evil that binds them. Lord, give us the strength and wisdom to see and do the right things tonight. To not bring harm where harm is not due and to bring mercy and relief where it is needed. This we pray to You, oh God, in Your name. Amen."

"Amen," we all repeated in unison.

In the parking lot, we all gathered around a black van with no windows on the side or back. Pastor Paul opened the side doors, and we all filed in, one by one. The interior of the van contained four captain's chairs in the middle and what appeared to be a digital command center in the back. Without a word, we all took our seats and the van was off, on its way south down the coastline.

Once we were on the road and had been on Route 35 for about five minutes,

Curtis turned to me, smiled and said, "This is pretty freakin' cool, isn't it?"

I looked around and nodded my head. "I guess so, but I don't even know what it all is."

"The back of the van is fully outfitted with a GPS system, radar, a computer with satellite uplink to the Internet, and the controls for the Hellfire system."

My eyebrows went up. "Hellfire?"

"Oh, yes," and Curtis' smile broadened even wider. "The Hellfire system is capable of projecting fire three hundred feet in any direction without harming anything between here and there and only affecting a ten foot radius." His smile was now so big I thought his face was going to crack.

"Have you ever used it?"

"No, but I got a good feeling about tonight." His face looked like a little kid about to get an ice cream cone.

"You love this stuff, don't you?" I asked with a wry smile.

"You know it, my friend." He looked at me and punched my fist in a sign of solidarity and to signify we were on the same page. I looked over at Natalie and found that she had her eyes closed, her head bowed, and was deep in prayer.

Her glossed pink lips were moving, but I couldn't hear what she was saying.

Then we returned to riding in silence as we crossed through Seaside Heights and onto Route 37. The sun was still in the sky, but it was getting low.

We were running out of daylight, and we needed to get there just at the right time between when the sun setting and night was coming into bloom. With things all quiet in the van again, my mind was racing from Sandy to Tyler to Caitlyn. I was having a problem reconciling all of this information. There were so many different things going through my head. I was so anxious to get there and save them. But the idea of not even trying to get Sandy was wearing on me. I didn't know if I could do it. If all three of them were huddled together, how could I not take Sandy? What had she done to deserve this fate? I still had love for her, but I had finally begun to accept her being gone. Conversely, I had not accepted the kids being gone and now the very real possibility that they were alive existed. I had seen Sandy, so I knew she was there. But the kids—I was going purely on faith with that, but it was a strong faith.

At that moment, I felt a touch on my shoulder. I looked over and it saw Natalie's deeply concerned face looking back at me.

"Take your troubles to the Lord. He will take the burden off your shoulders. These are things we were never meant to carry on our own."

It was as if she knew exactly what I was thinking and answered my internal question—what do I do? So I smiled and thanked her. Then I did something I had not done in years. I bowed my head and prayed.

Forty-five minutes after leaving the church in Point Pleasant, we arrived at the Beachwood Country club and pulled into the parking lot. The country club was about two miles from the school, but you could see it up the coastline of the river. It was a perfect spot to park the van and take off from. We all gathered outside the van, and Curtis took over.

"Okay, the boat is over there, ready to go." He pointed to a small wooden rowboat. "Here, everyone take a pair of these." He began handing out green tinted sunglasses. "These are new. Lightweight night-glasses. They're rechargeable and run off of small watch batteries, so they're light and easy to conceal, unlike goggles. However, they lack any of the features night-vision goggles have beyond allowing you to see better in the dark. There is no enhancement or targeting. But it is going to be dark down there, and we need to be able to see without flashlights. Okay, everybody in the boat."

We all started walking down the dock toward the boat, and the wind began whipping all around us. Curtis continued, "We'll be able to dock at the school's old dock and make our way around the front of the building. Remember, they use the old Naval Science entrance as their main way in and out, so be very careful when you pass it. You never know who will be about to come out.

Everybody armed and ready?"

Natalie and the pastor nodded, and I stared at him blankly. Were we really about to do this? Did I have any clue at all what I was doing? I quickly decided the answer to that was definitely "no." But I had God with me, and that was more than enough.

"Sam? You with us?" Curtis urged me.

"I'm with you, brother."

It had been years since I was on a boat on this river. The last time was just before graduation, when I took Sandy out in a catboat for a sail. The day was sunny, the breeze was light, and she was beautiful. We sailed to the other side of the river and back on that day, and thinking about it, it felt like it was only yesterday. But tonight, we were in a small wooden rowboat and traveling about thirty feet from the shore, doing our best to hug the shoreline without being overly conspicuous. But, hey, who would notice four people all dressed in black rowing up the Toms River at dusk in a wooden boat? Seems totally normal to me. In about ten minutes, we were staring at the old wooden dock of Admiral Farragut Academy. The sunlight had almost completely faded, but it was apparent that mooring at the dock would not be easy. The dock was severely decaying, which made us stop to re-evaluate our landing point.

"Curt," I started, "I'm having trouble seeing somewhere that's safe enough to tie up the boat and disembark. I don't think the planks will hold our weight."

He didn't answer right away, apparently assessing the situation as well. I could see his mind racing, trying to find a good place, but it just wasn't there.

Natalie and Pastor Paul were searching, too.

"What if we tied up over by the boat house and tried our luck there? The boathouse was shored up a lot stronger than the rest of the dock because the dock master had all sorts of equipment in there."

Curtis didn't respond to me; he looked over at the boathouse and nodded slowly.

"Sam, that's the best idea you've had in the past ten minutes. You think it's empty?"

"Hard to say—they practically gutted the school when it closed. Had a big auction and then people just started taking souvenirs. My guess would be anything substantial would have been removed, but we might find some small things in there." I paused and then added, "Heck, for all we know, kids might be using it as a hangout."

We started to move toward the boathouse, which still looked fairly sturdy from twenty feet away. The dock running from the boat house to shore, on the other hand, not so much.

"I somehow doubt anyone is using it to hang out in—how would they get there?" Natalie added in a loud whisper.

"The same way we are going to get out of there," Curtis said.

"And how is that?" asked Pastor Paul.

"The pilings are still perfectly strong, and the supports between them are sturdy as ever—it's just the planks that cross the supports that might have rotted.

We will have to walk across the supports to shore."

Natalie and I both nodded our heads in agreement, but Pastor Paul didn't look convinced.

"Really?" he began. "I'm not sure about this. I'm not really that good with the balance beam." The boat came up to the boat house, and Curtis stood to take hold of the piling.

"Sam, grab that piling, pull us in." I did. Curtis and I both tied the boat securely to the pilings.

"This puppy ain't going nowhere without us!" he exclaimed triumphantly— or at least as triumphantly as you exclaim anything in a hushed whisper. Pastor

Paul still didn't look very happy about the plan, but didn't say anything more about it.

"I'll go first, then Curtis, then the pastor, then Sam," Natalie said and deftly pulled herself up onto the crossbeam.

She stood and balanced herself with an agility and grace I had not seen in her before. It was impressive and very attractive to watch her shapely legs cross one in front of the other slowly but surely until she reached the next piling. She touched it lightly with one hand and swung her foot across it and onto the next crossbeam.

When Natalie was securely on the second beam, Curtis pulled himself onto the crossbeam without any resemblance to the swift and graceful motions that moved Natalie. Nonetheless, in a matter of moments he, too, was standing and making his way across the beam. Natalie was now almost to shore, and Curtis was just making it to the second crossbeam. It was time for Pastor Paul to start making his way over.

"Pastor?" I prompted him, but he didn't move.

"Sam, I am deathly afraid of heights. I don't think I can do it."

I took him by the shoulders and looked him straight in the eyes.

"Believe in the Lord; ask for His guiding hand. He will guide you and be with you, helping you every inch of the way. You can do this."

That small reassurance that he was not in this alone seemed to be all he needed to jumpstart his engine and get him moving. He slowly pulled himself onto the beam and moved surprisingly quickly to the piling. Natalie was already ashore and checking her gear while Curtis was only two lengths of the dock away from the shore, and Pastor Paul had paused at the first piling. I sat waiting for him to put his weight on the second crossbeam so I could grab on. I had to wait—I didn't want to shake the crossbeam and knock him off into the water. The sun had set, and there were only streaks of gold coming from the west end of the river. Daylight had vanished, and we weren't even on shore yet. We had to move faster.

Curtis reached shore, and finally the pastor began to make his way across the second crossbeam. There were ten in all, and I had a feeling this was still going to take awhile. When he was halfway across the second beam, I reached up and grabbed the piling, pulling myself up onto the crossbeam. It was dirty and heavily weatherworn. Much like the main building of the old campus, this area hadn't seen any maintenance lately and had been left to decay.

I began my trek across the beams, carefully putting one foot in front of the other until I reached the first piling. I took hold of it and looked around to take stock of where everyone was. Natalie and Curtis were on shore and looked like they were having a discussion about the building. Pastor was more than halfway to shore, so I continued onto the second crossbeam. I could feel the wind coming across the river and then swiftly up into my face. It was very brisk, and I began to feel a little off-balance. Focus, focus, focus. I had to focus. One foot in front of the other and slowly, very slowly, I made my way to the next piling. I looked up to find that Pastor Paul was almost there. I began to step up my pace, one slight step at a time. About three feet from the next piling, I heard a splash. I reached out for the piling for support and then looked up to see Pastor Paul in the water. Natalie and Curtis were rushing to his aid. But instead of flailing in the water helplessly, he was already standing up. The water ten feet from shore was only up to his mid-calf. He was making his way onto the beach, shaking his head in embarrassment. Seeing this made me a little more confident and I was able to quickly make my way to shore, knowing that if I fell in I would barely get wet. You'd think I'd have known that.

Finally on shore, I joined the rest of the team standing by the padlocked gate that led to the street across from Farragut Hall. I stood on the wrong side of the ten-foot tall chain link gate and stared through it at the building. What was once an ominous symbol of the oppression of slightly off-balance ex-military and petty officers now stood as an eerie reminder that no matter where you go or what you do, the past always comes back to find you when you are at your most vulnerable. The pale yellow and grey brothel-turned-hotel-turned-military- boarding school was now a hot spot for what could only be called a modern day chamber of sin.

There were no lights on in the building, but I could swear I saw people moving around in the well-secured windows. We couldn't see the door to the

Naval Science office from where we stood, but we could see the top of the stairs.

I could see people — or *Caelitus,* I guess — coming out into the ever-approaching night. I watched one, a woman with black hair. She couldn't have been older than 25, and she had a pretty face with high cheekbones. She appeared at the top of the steps and walked with a purposeful stride toward the road. Once she got to the road, she turned left and began running up Riverside Drive, and then she was gone. She ran so fast I couldn't see her anymore. The *Caelitus* could move at an incredible speed. It was almost mesmerizing to watch them, one after another, appearing from the steps and repeating the same movements.

"They're leaving the nest," Pastor Paul began. "Soon those who are going out to feed will all be gone, and there will only be a few left. Those are the ones who venture out in the daylight. They are the leaders of the clan. The most powerful among them."

"They're so graceful and fast," I said in an almost admiring tone.

"Exactly," said Curtis matter-of-factly, "and it makes them all the more dangerous. The ones left inside can kill you before you see them. The blood will be running down your shirt before you even realize that they slit your throat with their razor-sharp claws. That is why we have these."

And he produced small black boxes that he handed to each one of us.

"This is the vamprator."

"The what? That sounds more than vaguely pornographic, Curt."

"Vamprator—it vibrates like a cell phone anytime one of them gets within 20 feet of you. An incredibly useful gadget when you're stuck in the dark it just happens to have an incredibly silly name. Now, being inside the nest is going to make this thing go off like crazy, so just be aware when it does. It might be a false alarm. It detects pheromones that they give off. Usually, the pheromones serve to lull their victim into passive acceptance of the attention the vamp is showing them. You know, the same way that when a chick is into you, your pheromones keep her interest a hundred times stronger. This device picks the pheromones up and alerts you. It's not perfect, but better safe then dead."

"Yes, yes," Pastor Paul interjected, "but they won't necessarily be out to kill us tonight. Especially you, Sam. If their goal was to kill you, you'd be dead already. Either that or..." He trailed off and looked up.

"Or what?"

"Or you are the chosen one sent by God."

"What?" exclaimed Natalie, a little too loudly. We all ducked down out of sight. Curtis reached down and switched on our vamprators.

"Pastor, you can't be serious," she continued.

"What do you mean, chosen one?" I asked skeptically. I had never been chosen for anything worthwhile.

"It is written in the manuscripts that formed the *Pius Sacratus* centuries ago that one would come who would be immune to the charms of the *Caelitus*.

Not only that, but that no *Caelitus*—or any other species of vampire, for that matter—would be able to kill or turn the chosen one." I think the look on my face told him that I thought he hit his head when he fell in the water.

"You know that birthmark you have on your lower back?"

"Yeah, but wait... how did you know I have a birthmark on my back?"

"Because I also know that it is shaped like the fish symbol that has been used for centuries to symbolize the marking of the Christians." I had to think about it for a second, but I guess the birthmark did look like a fish. I hadn't thought about it before, but here I was on the beach of the Toms River, a couple hundred feet from my old high school-turned-vampire nest, being told that I was the chosen one to eradicate the world of vampires. It was kind of heavy.

"That doesn't make sense," started Natalie. And I picked up where she left off.

"How did you know about the birthmark? And how can I be the chosen one?"

Pastor Paul smiled slightly. "Sam, how do we know anything? The Lord just showed me your birthmark. He was telling me that you are, indeed, the chosen one. I caution you, this does not make you Superman. They can still catch you, hold you captive, and you can still be hurt in conventional ways. Your status only keeps you from being bitten or directly harmed by vampires. The Lord is with you and protects you from their evil."

Unbelievable was all I could mutter. It all made me want a bottle of Dr.

Jack Daniels. But he wasn't here now. It was only me. Me, the *Pius Sacratus,* and God. I was shaking my head, and I heard Pastor utter the words I didn't want to hear.

"It is time."

Before I knew what was happening, the lock was cut, the gate was open, and we were huddled across the street at the stairs that led to the building's main entrance. We all looked at each other, and Curtis motioned us to keep low and make our way around the sign on the corner of Riverside and Radnor Avenue.

The spot where all the vampires had started their run down Riverside.

The entrance we were trying to get to was down Radnor and at the back of the building. We would have to keep low and undetected to make it without alerting anyone that we were here. We kept low and made it to the sign, stopping to make sure no one had noticed us. The front of the building was quiet—everyone who was leaving must have already gone. I could hear the waves lightly lapping at the beach across the street and the trees rustling lightly.

Then I heard something else. I heard a distant and distressed, otherworldly voice.

"Sam."

I shook my head and rubbed my eyes, but there it was again.

"Sam. Hurry." Sandy's voice came through in an eerie monotone that sounded like three people speaking at the same time in a slightly different cadence. She inexplicably knew that I was here and was urging me on.

The others had already begun to make their way up Radnor Avenue towards a collection of bushes at the back corner of the building.

"Sam. Hurry. They are waiting for you."

The voice held me; I was frozen in place. I couldn't move. I was staring forward, watching the others take cover behind the bushes. I saw Natalie look back and notice I was still at the sign. She was waving me to hurry and follow them. Her lips were moving, but she was too far for me to hear what she was saying. Sandy 's pained voice spoke to me again.

"Sam, hurry, we are all waiting."

I shook my head and ran quickly to the bushes to catch up with the group.

"What were you doing?" Natalie asked insistently.

"Sandy knows we're here—she was talking to me."

That got everyone's attention. Pastor Paul looked at me with wide, disbelieving eyes.

"She told me they are waiting for me, and that I have to hurry."

"Incredible," was all Paul had to say.

"Then we shouldn't disappoint," Curtis began. "Okay, the door is just over there." He pointed to the alleyway that led to the tailor's door. "It doesn't look like anyone is around. Keep low, keep quiet, and keep moving. Let's go!"

One by one, we made our way to the alley. Curtis, Pastor Paul, Natalie, and then I went. Once inside the alley, Curtis began to examine the door. It looked like it was still the same old wooden door, just with a padlock on the outside. Curtis made quick work of the padlock and slowly opened the door. It creaked loudly as he opened it.

"Okay, everyone in. I'm going around to set the explosive on the other entrances, then back to the van. Sam, when everyone is out, radio me and I'll begin detonation of the explosives."

We all nodded in understanding. Then, donning our night-glasses, we shuffled into the dark room. I could see racks filled with clothing and tables that had piles of clothing scraps on them. This room looked as if it hadn't been used in years. The door shut behind us. This was it.

"There is a door, Sam."

Taking Sandy's cue, I led the team to the back of the room. I looked around and finally saw a door in the corner behind a rack of clothing.

"Nat, over there," I said, pointing to the rack.

"There it is!" she exclaimed. Natalie darted to the rack and moved the clothes out of the way. Pastor Paul and I followed to examine the door. I tried the handle. To my amazement, the handle turned, and the door opened into a dark and musty hallway. Hallway might have been an overstatement; it looked more like a path that led to the bowels of the building, it was lined with pipes and with pitch black. Good thing we had our night-glasses. None of us spoke as we went down the hall, descending into the darkness of the building. There was no sound beyond the shuffling of our feet.

"The path splits at the end — go to your right," Sandy's voice guided me.

We continued down the path, and about fifty feet later, I saw a wall coming up in front of us. But when we reached the wall, the path stopped. I didn't see any way to continue.

"Now what?" Natalie asked in a hushed voice.

"I don't know," I replied, "but we need to go to the right here." I began feeling all along the back wall, then on the right hand side until I felt something at the bottom.

"Something is down here, but I can't see it. It's too dark." It felt like a hand-hold, so I grabbed it and stuck my hand in about two inches and felt something solid. I pushed in hard, and the corner of the wall moved back slightly.

"Ah, look!" Pastor exclaimed and pushed on the corner. It gave way to the pressure, and we filed through the narrow opening into another corridor. The hall was dirt-lined, with nothing on the walls. It was much narrower than the other passageway and we had to walk in a line, one after the other. I led the way, with Natalie right behind me; I felt her hand on my shoulder, and I looked back.

"Just making sure you're still there," she said with a small smile. And then my vamprator started going off. It was vibrating like a telemarketer was calling, trying to sell me a timeshare. I stopped and started looking around, but I couldn't see anything.

"What's wrong, Sam?" Natalie asked.

"The vamprator—it's going crazy."

"Mine isn't doing anything," she replied.

"Neither is mine," commented Pastor Paul in a distracted voice.

I gave the immediate area another look and then kept going. As we continued, I heard Natalie's vamprator start to vibrate, and then Pastor Paul's.

"We must be close to something."

"I think you are right, Pastor."

I slowed the pace as we approached a door that had a soft glow spilling out from beneath it. I turned, putting one finger to my lips in a sign of silence to

Natalie and Pastor Paul. It didn't occur to me until I had done so that this was a futile gesture—if there were vampires on the other side of that door, they could hear us anyway with their acute sense of hearing.

When we reached the door, Natalie gently pushed me aside and crouched down to the floor. She reached inside her backpack and pulled out a small mirror on a handle, just like what you might see at the dentist's office. She slid it under the door, moving it back and forth slowly until she was satisfied.

"Doesn't seem to be anyone in there. Looks like a large open room with some lanterns burning on the walls." We both nodded to show our understanding, and she tried the door handle. It turned easily, and she slowly pushed the door open into the room.

The room was large, perhaps half a football field in size. There were many wooden tables throughout the large cafeteria-looking room. Some of the tables had unlit candles on them while others were completely bare. The walls were hung with what appeared to be old oil lamps, which were lit and giving off a soft amber glow. The light was just enough to see, but not enough to be able to make out anything specific at any distance. There were exits to the left, right and center. None of them had doors, and they appeared to lead to other hallways. I looked from one to the other, trying to discern the right way to go.

Where was Sandy now? I needed some direction, now more than ever.

The vamprators were still buzzing violently, and I reached down and turned mine off. Natalie and Pastor Paul followed suit.

"So," Natalie began, "which way to go?" She stood to my left with her hands on her hips, looking at the tables with some interest. She took her hands off her hips, walked over to one of the tables, and picked up a glass. She turned it over in her hands, noticing the traces of a rich red liquid that had pooled at the bottom of the glass.

"Any bets on whether this is wine?"

"I somehow doubt it," Paul responded with a pained expression on his face.

"Which way?" The words slowly rolled out of my mouth; I had no idea.

"Gang, I think this might be where we split up. Nat, you head left, Pastor you go right, and I'll split the difference in the middle."

"Right," said Natalie, "meet back here in 20 minutes?"

"Agreed," Paul and I said at the same time.

"I think we should go one at a time, though," Pastor offered. "That way we can make sure the others are okay, at least for two minutes or so."

We agreed to this—first Natalie would go, then Paul, then I would go by myself. We all approached the hall to the left and entered slowly. We peered down the hall together and saw that the oil lamps continued to light the way. The passage continued to descend slightly, with steps about fifty feet down.

"Okay," she sighed, "here I go." And Natalie slowly began creeping down the hall. She looked back about ten feet away and gave us a thumbs-up. Paul and I returned the thumbs-up and walked back into the room towards the hall to the right. We slowly approached the hall, peered down and saw what appeared to be a mirror image of Natalie's hall, complete with steps about fifty feet away.

The pastor began making his way slowly then looked back, nodding his head to indicate he was okay.

Now it was my turn.

Approaching the entrance to the hallway, I began to notice that this one looked very different from the others. It was darker, barely lit at all. Finally, I stood at a doorway that looked very different from the two Natalie and Pastor

Paul had gone down. This doorway didn't lead to a hall—at least not directly— but stood at the stop of a tall stairway that appeared to be lit by very few oil lamps. I couldn't see the bottom of the stairway, so I put my glasses back on to try and see further down before I began my journey into the depths of this hellhole. The glasses didn't help very much—apparently they weren't powerful enough to see that far.

I was a little troubled that Sandy had led me this far and then seemed to abandon me. Again. It made me wonder, who was Sandy trying to help? Was it really me? Or the kids? Or maybe Khayman? Natalie had said that when Emily was abducted, the Khaymans had really come for me. Maybe Sandy was leading me directly into a trap that would only end up with me becoming one of them. But Pastor Paul had said I was immune to that—or so he thought. Feeling like I had no other choice, I began my descent into the darkness that awaited me. I took the stairs one at a time, slowly and deliberately, with one hand on the wall to the right of me. About ten steps down, the glasses started to bring more of the stairway into focus. And all I saw were more steps. How far down did these steps go? I only had twenty minutes to search and meet back in the main room, and I didn't see any end to these stairs in sight.

But as I kept going down, step-by-step, I began to hear noises. Strange scratching and shuffling noises were coming from below me. I was walking right into the disturbing sounds. The deeper I got, the louder they got, and the oil lamps were now either not lit or not nonexistent.

After fifty or so steps, I could see the bottom. I was about halfway down the steps now, and I had the feeling that I was not alone. I couldn't see anyone or anything but steps and the floor, but there were definitely others here with me.

I broke out in a sweat in spite of the cold air that began to swirl around me the deeper I went into the vampire nest. I reached into my vest and pulled out the gun.

And then I was on the last step. I stopped for a moment, realizing I had no idea how long it had taken me to get here. I looked from one side to the other and still did not see anyone, but straight ahead, about three hundred feet at the other side of the room, was a faint glow of light. I stepped down off the step and before my foot hit the floor, I was blindsided by someone... or something? It hit me from the left, square in the shoulder, and knocked me from my feet. I dropped the gun and heard it skid across the concrete. I looked feverishly around, trying to find my assailant.

I didn't move for a long moment, but my attacker didn't come back. Maybe they went to tell others? No matter what, someone knew I was here. I had to hurry. I looked around for the gun but couldn't see it anywhere; I was going to have to forget it and just head for the door. In an instant, I was on my feet and running across the large expanse toward the light, afraid whatever it was that had knocked me down was going to continue after me. I had seen how fast these things were and knew that if I couldn't see them, I had no chance against them. I got to the door and slammed up against it, running so fast that I was unable to stop. The collision made a loud thud against the door, and I heard frantic movement behind it. Dammit, why didn't I just ring the doorbell, too? But, fearful of whoever—or whatever—knocked me down, I flung the door open with complete disregard for what was waiting for me on the other side. At least I would be able to see with the light from behind the door.

I flung the door open and froze. I stood with my mouth wide open, not believing my eyes. I removed my glasses and heard them hit the floor, having no idea where they landed. There, standing before me, was my dead wife, Sandy... except she didn't look all that dead. She looked absolutely beautiful, the light of the oil lamps playing on her curly blonde hair. Her skin was porcelain, much lighter than it had been before, and her lips were a deep red, as if she had just had a glass of cabernet. So, aside from that, she didn't look dead. It's all in the details, apparently. Neither one of us moved; we just stared at each other.

"Finally, you're here. I've been waiting," she said without moving her lips.

"I knew you would come. There is much danger and very little time, so you must hurry." Her voice was clear and had a strong sense of urgency behind it.

I was not sure how to answer her. But before I could figure it out, she looked over her shoulder and stepped back to reveal Tyler and Caitlyn lying in what looked like plush red sofa chairs. They appeared to be asleep. I began walking toward them and stopped when I reached Sandy.

"What..." I stammered.

"There will be more time for explanations some other time; for now you need to get them out of here and to a place where they will be safe and happy.

They have been in stasis since we disappeared. It's the air here—there are pheromones in the air that keep them asleep. They have no knowledge or memory of this place, only the accident. Once you get them out, they will wake up within hours." This time she was speaking through her mouth, so I could hear it and see her luscious lips moving. They were so big and red; they beckoned me to kiss them.

"I don't...." I looked directly into her cold, dead black eyes, "I don't understand; what is going on here? Why are you here? How did you get involved with Khayman?" Suddenly, the idea of romance wasn't so appealing as I remembered where I was and what I was doing.

"Sam." Her facial expression changed to reflect her pleading tone. "You must take them, now! There is no time for explanations or apologies. You have already been here too long; they know you are here and will come for you... and them." She looked at the sleeping children.

"I can't just take them and go; where is Emily? And I *need* to know what happened."

"Emily?" She looked surprised. "You mean the F.B.I. agent who was in the cottage?"

"Yes, her."

"I don't know; she was there when I went to you. I didn't know what to think, so I just left her there. She's not here, Sam. If she were, I'd know about it."

"But the blood on the door. It looked like she had been taken."

"Yes, I put the blood on the door. The blood was to keep other vampires away—the mark signified that there was nothing to feed on inside so they would pass you by."

"Then what happened to Emily?"

"I don't know; this may sound stupid, but did you call her?"

So here I was in the depths of the ground in Pine Beach, talking with my undead wife about the girl I just had sex with, while the girl I was falling in love with was searching a different part of the lair. And strangely enough, this wasn't awkward at all. It didn't seem strange or weird. I guess that, in and of itself, should have told me something. I found the lack of emotion I felt for Sandy right now amazing. It was so apparent to me that she wasn't Sandy anymore, not the woman I loved, not the woman I married. She was someone... no, some*thing* else.

"Sandy, I can't carry them myself. I have to go back and get Natalie or Paul for help. And I need you to explain this to me; explain to me how you got here, why Khayman took you and the kids. I've wasted a lot of time blaming myself for what happened only to find out that you aren't even dead."

"But Sam, I am no longer alive. I am undead." She took my hand in hers; it was as cold as the outside of a car in the middle of winter. There was no color to her skin and no warmth to her touch. She placed my hand on her left breast, and I could not feel a heart beating beneath.

"I have so much to tell you, so much to explain and apologize for." Sandy spoke earnestly and from her heart, or whatever you would call it in her case.

"There will be time for that later, in another time and in another place. But you must go now; I will help you carry them. Please!" she pleaded and bent over to pick up Caitlyn. I grabbed Tyler and followed her out the door towards the stairs.

She stopped about ten feet in, and I could barely see her. I didn't have the glasses anymore and was relying solely on the light from the room.

"Someone is here," she told me in my head. Then she resumed moving towards the stairs.

"I told them to get out of here. They did leave, but they will be back with reinforcements in moments—we must hurry!"

"I am going as fast as I can!" I said irritably.

We reached the stairs, and she started to pick up speed. I had to run to try and keep up, but Tyler was heavy and I was getting tired. Sandy was still several steps ahead of me and stopped about ten steps from the top at the last plateau before the steps led into the room.

"Stop! Someone is in the common room; there are both humans and undead. This isn't good." I could hear the concern in her unearthly voice.

I finally caught up to her.

"Who?"

"It's Natalie and Paul. And there are some vampires with them, but I can't tell what is going on, only that Natalie and Paul are distressed in some way."

I laid Tyler down gently on the ground and began going up the stairs.

"Stop!" she said loud enough for the neighbors to hear. "Are you crazy?"

"I can't just stand here; I have to see what is going on. It sounds like they're in trouble. If they are, then I have to help. It's the only way."

"Sam, if they are, it is already too late."

"Sandy, I think you underestimate us all. Stay here, protect the kids. I'll be back." I could hear sounds of a struggle as I crept closer to the top of the stairs. I took out the silver crucifix from my vest, preparing to do battle, reached the top, and walked through the entrance.

"Okay, let's get it on!" I exclaimed loudly to get everyone's attention. All the motion in the room stopped. I saw Pastor Paul bound and gagged at one end of the room and Natalie bound and gagged at the other. They stopped struggling to get loose and looked my way. Paul looked as though he had been taken easily, with little damage. But Natalie had clearly put up a fight and looked worse for the wear. She had a cut above her eyebrow, and it was bleeding around the edges of her right eye. Her face was caked in a layer of dirt, and the top of her jumpsuit had several nasty-looking blood soaked tears. She looked at me pleadingly and then looked to the vampires at a table, who were going through what looked to be her backpack. There were five of them, and they were all looking directly at me. I began walking toward them purposefully. I heard Natalie scream under her gag and felt something approaching from behind; I quickly turned and plunged the crucifix deep into the vampire who was in mid-air, about to land squarely on my back. The force of him coming knocked me flat on my back and he landed squarely on me, pushing the blunt edge of the crucifix into my chest. Damn, that hurt like hell! That was definitely going to leave a mark, but I was okay. I shoved him off me and spun to my feet, crucifix in hand.

The five of them were now on their feet, standing in a line, licking their bloody lips and staring at me with such intensity that I could feel their bloodlust.

But they weren't going to be getting any of my blood, not tonight. They began to close on me all at once, and I wished I still had the gun. I heard footsteps behind me, and the approaching vampires froze. One of them stopped mid-stride and almost fell over. The smell of them reached me, and it was putrid.

"I don't want to have to destroy you, but I will. You will leave him alone."

Sandy's voice was strong and commanding from behind me.

Then the middle one spoke. "You protect this human intruder?" he asked incredulously.

"You will let them go, all of them," she said and came up behind me, depositing my gun in the back pocket of my pants as if she had read my mind.

Way to go, Sandy! Then out of the corner of my eye, I saw Sandy flash over to

Natalie and untie her. She didn't linger, but I saw them exchange a quick glance with each other.

"You traitor!" the one on the left end spat out. "I will personally see to it the Khayman finds out about this!"

"You do what you have to do; I am serving my sentence. There is no reason for my children and these people to serve it with me." And she began to flash to Pastor Paul but was intercepted by the middle vampire. He was, apparently, the one in charge of this little band of vamps. He grabbed her by her throat and held her up. She was clearly shocked by this, but it didn't appear that she could do anything about it. Natalie began running to her but was jumped by two of the others. She spun and landed a kick into one of them, knocking him back. But before she could spin again, the other vampire was on her back. I ran to help Natalie but was broadsided by one of the remaining two vamps. He had me down on the floor and was about to sink his fangs into my throat when he stopped suddenly, a confused look on his face. He looked at me as if I were a piece of steak he wanted to eat only to realize at the last moment that the meat was rancid. I guess God was on my side, after all. I took the opportunity to deliver an elbow to his chin and he fell back, clutching his mouth, blood spilling from his lips. The other vampire was on me quickly, but I was able to spin the crucifix on him, and it landed in the side of his neck. He fell away and grabbed the crucifix, then quickly let it go as the flesh on his hands began to burn like the flesh surrounding the wound on his neck.

I quickly checked on Sandy and Natalie. The vampire now had Sandy pinned to the wall by her neck, which was apparently a mistake. She used the leverage from the wall to deliver a strong kick to his stomach, and he dropped her hard on the ground. She lay there for a moment, rubbing her neck, before getting back to her feet.

Natalie was furiously trying to get the vampire off her back. I could see he had pulled up her hair and was bearing his teeth about to bite her. I pulled the gun from my back pocket, took aim, and fired a round. It struck the vampire in the shoulder and he screeched in pain, falling from Natalie's back onto the hard floor. He was writhing around in agonizing pain, but not dead.

Natalie ran to the table and reclaimed her backpack. She walked quickly back to the injured vamp and drove a silver stake into his chest, killing him instantly. His body went limp, and blood pooled underneath him so quickly that Natalie had to jump back. I ran over to Pastor Paul and began to untie him when a booming voice came from the door the far hallway.

"If you all want to live, stop right where you are."

There stood Max Khayman, the head of the Khayman clan. And he was staring directly at me. I finished freeing Pastor and stood to return the hard stare.

"Khayman," I said.

"Sam Shepard, what a wonderful family reunion this is. Sandy, please tell me you didn't kill any of your brothers here."

"No, Max. I didn't. But Sam needs to take Tyler and Caitlyn out of here.

They don't belong here, and you know it."

Khayman's expression changed to a cold, hard look.

"Don't tell me what I know. The only reason you were allowed to live at all is because I enjoy screwing you and feeding off you. Your children will grow and become *Caelitus* just like you." He smiled, an evil and knowing smile. Sandy looked down at her feet, appearing embarrassed and ashamed of where she was and what was happening to her.

"I'm taking my children. Whatever Sandy did, she is paying for it, but I won't allow my children to stay here," I said firmly and flexed the hand with the gun in it. Khayman paid the gun some regard—apparently he hadn't seen it before. He began walking slowly towards me. Natalie lunged for him, but he swatted her away like a fly, and she hit the wall hard. She wasn't out, but she was definitely down. The two remaining vampires fell in step behind their leader, and when they reached Sandy, they all stopped. Khayman put a finger under her chin to left her face up to him; she appeared to be crying.

"You will be punished," he said simply, and nodded to the two behind him.

They stepped up and grabbed her by each arm and began leading her back the way Khayman came in. She didn't appear to fight them.

"Pastor," I whispered, "Tyler and Caitlyn are on the stairs. I will handle

Khayman. Go get them. Get them out of here." He nodded and started to walk towards the stairs.

"Where you are you going, Padre? Not staying for the party? I don't think that is very nice." And in a flash, he was in front of Pastor Paul and had knocked him to the ground.

"Sit, stay; this is going to be very entertaining for you."

Max Khayman turned his attention back to me now that the pastor had, at least temporarily, been subdued. He walked slowly toward me. I could see that Natalie was starting to stir and the pastor was slowly getting to his feet. None of this seemed to concern Khayman in any way, as he was now fully focused on me and approaching fast.

"Stop right there, Khayman." I raised the handgun and pointed it at his chest. His expression changed to one of amusement.

"Oh, no." He raised his hands and looked up mockingly. "Don't shoot, you big bad vampire slayer man." He dropped his hands and looked at me flatly.

"Who do you think you are? Buffy? She was way more attractive then you. You can't kill me. And I would have killed her, right after I violated her in many, many bad ways." He smiled. "You, I won't kill you; just make you suffer." In the blink of an eye, he was upon me, and with a flick of his wrist he knocked the gun from my hand.

Before I could react, his face screwed up with pain and surprise. His hand went slowly to his back, where he pulled out a dagger. He held it up in front of his face and tossed it aside with little regard.

"You are going to have to excuse me—I have to deal with a small issue."

He turned and I saw Pastor Paul behind him, holding a small silver crucifix at arm's length towards Khayman. Khayman swatted the crucifix out of his hand, but Natalie came at him from his blind side and delivered a swift kick to his side.

He felt it, but it didn't take him down.

"Sam, go!" yelled Natalie, "We've got him!"

It seemed my partners didn't follow instructions well, so I sprinted towards the stairs, picking up the gun along the way. I found Tyler and Caitlyn on the landing. I bent down, picked up little Caitlyn, and positioned her in a fireman's- style hold on one shoulder, then Tyler on the other. I heard Natalie cry out in pain, while the pastor was chanting some Bible verses. I took the steps as fast as I could and saw that in spite of the cry of pain, it looked like Natalie and Paul were at least keeping Khayman occupied.

I got to the door and stopped, looking back just in time to see Natalie go flying against the wall again. Khayman turned on Pastor Paul and picked him up by his neck. I put Tyler and Caitlyn down safely in the hall and turned back into the room. I pointed the gun toward Khayman.

"Now, Padre, you have become more than a simple annoyance." Pastor's arms and legs were flailing helplessly in the air. I took aim and fired a shot. But I missed Khayman and hit the wall in the back of the room. He looked toward me, and he looked angry. He dropped Pastor Paul to the ground and was on top of me in a flash. He delivered a punch to my midsection that doubled me over, and I couldn't breathe.

"You poor, weak human. Don't you understand that you are little more to me than a selection on my buffet table?" He grabbed me by the hair and dragged me back into the middle of the room, delivering a vicious kick to the side of my head. I felt consciousness slipping from my grasp: My vision was blurry and I was having trouble moving. I could feel blood trickling from my nose and my ear. I couldn't hear anything out of the ear where he'd kicked me. In a blurry blob, I saw Khayman drop to his knees beside me.

"And now, you become the appetizer before I go fuck your wife. What do you think about that? Oh, don't worry; she likes it. You should hear her moan with pleasure when I drink from her. Oh, and I know what you are thinking. You didn't see any bite marks on her neck, did you? No, of course you didn't. That's not where I feed from." Although my vision was blurred and hazy, I could see the wicked smile on his face when he threw his ugly head back and laughed loudly. I picked my head up in time to see his fist coming down on me. I heard the cartilage in my nose crunch like a cracker, and the blood flowed freely as I fell over onto my side. That's when I realized I still had the gun in my hand.

"I know what else you are thinking, little man. You are thinking, *Oh, I am the chosen one; you can't hurt me.* But tell me, oh chosen one, how does your face feel? Hurts like hell, doesn't it? That's only the beginning. And believe me, I can drink from you—it just won't turn you. I can drink from you and you will hurt like you have never hurt before; pain will stab your heart with each gush of blood that I suck from your withered and weakened body. I'll leave you alone for a couple of days, let you build your strength back up a little, then I'll do it all over again. It will never end, until the day you die from natural causes. Or maybe it will be a heart attack." He laughed finding himself amusing. "So, you see, Sandy has it pretty good. She can enjoy being screwed by me and is able to experience the pleasure of me feeding off her every day... forever. But for you, because you can't be turned, the feeding will be torture. And the God thatyou love so much, the one that is protecting you from becoming one of us. The pain will all be because He is protecting you from our power. If you are wondering about your friends over there... don't worry, I'll turn them and make them bloodthirsty minions who will do my bidding. And since I know you can't wait to experience it, I'm going to stop wasting everyone's time and take a nice big bite."

I raised the gun just off the ground and pulled the trigger. The round hit

Khayman's knee and blew it to pieces, blood flying everywhere. His scream was deafening to my good ear. I rolled onto my other side, shielding myself from the horrible sound.

At that moment, the first explosion rocked the building. Khayman stopped screaming and looked up at the ceiling as particles of dirt and rock shook loose.

Natalie was shaking her head and trying to adjust her sense of balance. I watched her struggle to get to her feet. She went over to the pastor and helped him up. Once he was on his feet, they came over to me. They were both hurt, but in better shape than I was. Natalie helped me to my feet.

"Are you okay, Sam?"

"No," I answered, "but I'll make it. Get the kids; get out of here now!" I yelled.

Khayman saw us and tried to get up when the second and third explosions went off. Curtis must have been setting them off at specific intervals. Once I cleared my head a little bit, I turned back to the doorway. Pastor and Natalie

went through before me, and I turned to look at Khayman lying on the ground, holding his knee.

"This is for Sandy," I said with no emotion in my voice and shot him in the other knee.

"Now, you get to lay there and suffer while the building comes down on top of you." As I shut the door to the room I saw several vampires running into the room to Khayman's aid. Natalie had already picked up Caitlyn and was on her way up the incline toward the opening in the wall. Pastor just about had Tyler in his arms when I got to him.

"Come on, Sam; let's get out of here before anything else blows up." I nodded, and we began the ascent behind Natalie. She moved quickly and got to the opening well ahead of us. I watched her disappear into the tailor's shop.

Pastor and I were about halfway up the hall when the next two explosions went off. We both looked at each other, I grabbed his shoulder to help him with

Tyler, and we sped up our pace the best we could. We were both hurt badly and struggling to make it up the passageway. When we finally reached the opening, smoke was everywhere, and the door at the entrance was wide open. We began coughing violently. Natalie and Caitlyn were nowhere to be seen.

"They must have made it outside," I yelled in Pastor's ear. He nodded his head, but it was hard to see anything besides Paul, Tyler and the light from the doorway.

"Go to the light, Pastor!"

He started toward the door and ran headlong into a table, yelling out in pain. I took Tyler from him and pushed him around the table toward the door.

We were about ten feet from the door when he suddenly went down.

"Come on! Get up!" I yelled. But he was on the ground, coughing violently.

"I—" *cough* "—can't—" *cough* "—Go! GO!—" *cough*.

He was lying on the ground, and I couldn't reach down to help him up with Tyler in my arms.

"I'll be back!" I yelled, and he nodded in understanding. I looked up for the light again, but the smoke had increased in thickness and I had trouble finding it.

I started coughing and realized that I had no idea what the smoke was doing to

Tyler. I didn't know where the door was, but I had to get out, so I decided to just keep going in the same direction. I would hit to door eventually, but how would I get back in for Pastor? I said a quick prayer, asking for aid and guidance, and continued towards where I thought the door was.

"SAM! Where are you?" I heard Natalie's voice coming from the door. I was close. I turned slightly, relieved that my prayer had just been answered.

"I'm here, I'm coming!" I started to feel heat from behind me. The shop must have caught fire from the explosion of the Naval Science entrance.

"Sam! This way!"

Then I saw the blood that had colored the skin surrounding her eye. I saw the cuts on her face and it was the most beautiful sight I could imagine at that moment. The light from out on the formation blocks just outside the tailor shop door was silhouetting the lovely shape of her head. Natalie's smile beamed through the smoke, and she reached to help me through the doorway. Once I was out, I ran to the grass and fell to my knees, coughing violently and placing Tyler down next to Caitlyn on the grass about fifty feet from the now-burning building. Sirens were wailing in the distance. It wouldn't be long before the fire trucks arrived—the volunteer firehouse was only a few blocks away.

"Where is Pastor Paul?" asked Natalie with alarm in her voice.

"Still—" —*cough* "—inside! He fell about ten or fifteen feet from the door.

I couldn't pick him up then; I have to go back!" Just then the van came screeching into the parking area and Curtis jumped out.

"Curt, Pastor is still inside the tailor shop." He didn't say anything, but quickly took action. He ran to the van and grabbed what looked like a gas mask, putting it on as he ran into the burning building. Moments later the fire trucks came wailing onto the formation blocks. Some of the trucks continued around to the front of the building on the grass. After what seemed like forever, Curtis emerged from the flame-engulfed building with Pastor Paul on his arm. Curtis was now coughing, and Pastor had the mask on. They both seemed okay, if not a little toasted.

"I got him! He's going to be okay!" Curtis yelled over the amalgam of clashing sounds.

I looked up to see Farragut Hall burning from within, all the wood and dangerous asbestos polluting the air with a huge plume of black smoke. That vision would be imprinted in my memory forever.

The next thing I knew we were surrounded by firemen, policemen and emergency medics asking questions. It seemed like the questions would never end. But we were all here, and we were all okay.

And then I passed out.

March 17th

I awoke the next day in the hospital with Natalie waiting at my bedside.

When she saw I was awake, she leaned forward and grasped my hand. Her eyes were lined with concern, but her lips were smiling.

"Sam, you're awake," was all she said, but the sound of her voice felt like
a big hug.

"I'm awake, but I feel like I've been hit by a truck."

"Doctors say you have three broken ribs, a broken nose, and a punctured eardrum. They treated you for smoke inhalation and sedated you."

I tried to move and was immediately halted by the searing pain in my side.

"Sam, lie still; you're going to be here for a few days. And those ribs are going to be very sore."

"Tyler and Caitlyn?"

"They're fine; they woke up about two hours after arriving at the hospital.

They don't remember anything about...." She hesitated, trying to decide how to say it. "Well, you know."

"I know. Sandy told me they wouldn't remember anything besides the accident."

"Yeah, they seem to be okay, but they keep asking where Mommy and Daddy are. I told them you were here, but I don't know what to tell them about Sandy. That seemed to hold them for now, but they want to see you." Natalie's expression was troubled; she was really conflicted.

"That's probably for the best for now. I'll have to explain it to them, when I can."

Natalie sat with a sad, reflective expression on her face.

"Did they find anything? Bodies? Were they asking questions?"

"The police think we got a phone call telling us where the kids were and that it was some kind of trap to kill us all. I'm sure they will be by to ask you questions, but they seem satisfied about Tyler and Caitlyn, and mostly about the fire. So far they haven't found any bodies, but they're still sorting through the wreckage of the building."

I looked at her with the question in my eyes. "It's...?"

"It's completely gone—they couldn't put the fire out, so they let it burn out."

For a moment I stared off over her shoulder, realizing that the building, the legacy of the school, my wife—it was all gone. And lying here in this hospital bed, I had no assurance that the evil infecting the underworld of Pine Beach was actually destroyed. I felt like I had to go there, had to see what was left, see what remained of the evil rooted there for who knows how long. I would get there, in due time.

"It's going to take some time for them to clear the debris. But I'm sure they'll find the bodies, or at least some semblance of bodies. Just give it time,

Sam. Everything will be work out the way it is supposed to. The doctors said they're going to release Pastor Paul this afternoon. He's okay; the smoke really got to him, though. Who knows what was in the air of that building that we all inhaled."

And she smiled a lovely, reassuring smile.

"What about you; are you okay?" I asked, trying to look her over for any obvious injuries aside from the stitches. She kept smiling.

"Just these—" she looked up at the stitches and rolled her eyes "—and my head hurts like hell. But I'm all right. Mostly worried about you." Her smile turned a little bashful. She seemed to care about me quite a bit.

"Sam," she began as something darkened her face, "I need to ask you, about..." She paused for a long moment, and I took in the strange combination of beauty and concern. "...your drinking. I don't want to see you fall back on the whiskey; there is so much here for you. I'm here for you." She flashed a questioning smile at me.

"Natalie, I have found my God, my children, and the answer to my prayers—you."

She smiled, leaned over, and kissed me softly on the lips. She tasted like cherries.

I smiled. "New lip gloss?"

Curtis came into the room, also smiling.

"Sammy!" *Sammy*? How did this trend get started?

"Hey Curt, what's happening?" I watched my old friend come into my hospital room.

"I just came by to see how you were feeling, and tell you the kids are doing fine and that it doesn't look like they're going to find anything in the ruins of the school. Don't know what to say."

Natalie turned to him. "How can you say that? They haven't even started looking?"

"That's just it, Nat. They aren't going to look. The police said they were just going to clean it up and that was it—they had no reason to search the ruins."

"No reason? Two children were found, we look like we've been through a war zone, and a building is burned to the ground, but they don't have any reason to search?"

He shrugged and kept on smiling.

"So, we may never know what happened to Khayman. And to Sandy," I said flatly without any inflection.

"I don't know, Sam," Curtis began. "I really don't think anything, living or undead, could have survived that. I'm just sorry I didn't get a chance to use

Hellfire on the place!"

I sighed deeply and shook my head at him. "Has anyone heard anything about Emily?"

Natalie and Curtis looked at each other before Natalie answered.

"No, nothing yet."

"Sandy said Emily wasn't there, that they didn't take her. She said that she put the blood on my door to keep other vamps out. No harm was done to her. So what happened to Emily?"

"I don't know," said Curtis, "maybe you should call Becky. Maybe they have some information."

The words were barely out of his mouth when there was a soft knock at the door.

"Anyone home? Can I come in?" came a soft, familiar voice. And through the door walked Emily Noble, all in one piece and looking as lovely as ever in a black suit that accentuated her small but shapely frame.

"You okay, Sam? I heard about the incident in Pine Beach and knew it had you written all over it. Then the home office contacted me and told me they heard I had been kidnapped and to contact Rebecca Sloane at Point Pleasant Police. So I gave her a call to let her know that I was fine. As soon as Becky told me what happened at the inn, combined with the incident in Pine Beach... I knew something bad had happened. I was very worried. Becky told me where they had taken you, and I came right over."

"I'm alright, Emily, but what happened to you? Why did you just leave like that?"

She looked taken aback by the question. "I slept and then left to go home.

I—," she stammered a little here and looked at Natalie. "I didn't think you'd really want to see me or, you know, talk to me. There was so much that happened."

She was blushing now, a nice shade of red. It really went well with the eye shadow she had on. She was looking at Natalie and seemed to go silent.

I smiled, glad to see she was okay and not sure how to explain any of this to her.

"I'm just glad you didn't get abducted by an evil clan of vampires, that's all." I smiled.

"An evil clan of what?" Based on the expression on her face, Emily was not expecting me to say that. And Natalie, Curtis and I found that pretty darned funny. The three of us broke out in a loud fit of laughter. Emily did not seem amused, so I took on the task of explaining to her what we found and what had happened.

Epilogue
April 1ˢᵗ

The weather had finally started to warm up a little bit. It was sunny, a little over 70 degrees and simply beautiful. We decided to spend the day at the beach, but not the ocean—the river. The wind was whipping at my back as I tacked to port and watched the splash of water come over the bow. I watched Tyler was lean over the rail and run his hand in the water, laughing hysterically.

Caitlyn came up on deck with a huge smile on her face and ran over to me seizing my leg in a big hug. I still almost couldn't believe they were back.

"Daddy, I'm hungry. When's lunch?"

"We're going to drop anchor and have lunch in a few minutes, sweetie."

"Okay, Daddy." And she ran over to her brother and joined him with her hand in the water, too.

The boat kept running straight as we cruised past the site of the old

Farragut Hall. I looked starboard and took in the sight of the ruins. They had cleared the wreckage off the site. They found the rooms below, but nothing was in them beyond tables and chairs. No bodies and no evidence of foul play. And in the end, the authorities found nothing of any interest to them. So they were beginning the process of filing it in and covering it up.

And it was then, at that very moment looking over the site where I recovered my children and found closure on the death of my wife, that it hit me.

God had blessed me in more ways than I could have ever asked for. It was that moment that I looked skyward and uttered the words that had escaped me until now.

"You have found me Lord, and I accept you, Jesus Christ, as my savior and God. I accept the mission You have placed upon my shoulders and thank

You for including me in Your grand plan."

I knew that God had put me in this place for a good reason. I was here to erase the plague of the vampire from the world, and I was more sure of that then

I had been of anything ever before. My life had changed forever: No more liquor, no more crass womanizing. I was a different man in a different world. Just like the sands on the beaches of the Toms River, time would go on, and I had to be there; I had to be pure to make sure the evil did not spread.

I could hear Kenny Chesney's "Summertime" coming from below deck and began singing along.

Two bare feet on the dashboard
Young love in an old Ford
Cheap shades and a tattoo
And a Yoo-Hoo bottle on the floorboard

Kenny Chesney always seemed to get me.
"Honey, are we ready to eat lunch yet?"
"Yes, let's drop anchor. Kids, come help Daddy!"

I still didn't know why things happened the way they did. I had no idea why Khayman was after Sandy. But as Natalie came up on deck with the tray of sandwiches, all I could do was look up and thank God for all the blessings He had given me. I would find the answers at the time I am meant to know them. , I know now more than ever that life can be fluid rising and falling like water lapping on the shore. With the wind whipping her hair across her face, Natalie and I exchanged glances, and we both knew that our work was not done here.

Not by a long shot.

Special Sneak Peak at Towering Pines Volume One: Room 509 by Bruce A. Sarte. Towering Pines is currently available in Paperback, Kindle, Nook, Smashwords and iBookstore formats.

For more information about Towering Pines visit bruceasarte.com or buckscountypublishing.com.

Prologue

October 30, 1984

Scott Paulsen stood on the edge overlooking the campus watching the Toms River shimmer like black ice in the moonlight. From fifty feet up, the moonlight hit the water and reflected into his eyes so he could barely see anything else. For the third night this week Scott found himself here. After evening inspection and lights out, he put his head down on the pillow and began his nightly ritual of counting backwards in French from 100 to fall asleep. As usual, the last thing he remembered was reaching quarante cinq and then he fell into a deep sleep. The next thing he knew he was standing in this spot at exactly the same time each night.

Scott Paulsen's return to consciousness was the same on each of these evenings. His eyes moved from port to starboard taking in Dodge Hall, the tennis courts, the football field and finally he could see the gym through the towering pine trees. With a startling suddenness the wind hit him hard in the face. The force of the wind stole his breath and caused him to blink his eyes rapidly. Just when he thought he as going to pass out the wind died down allowing him to inhale deeply. He looked up into the moonlight and stared for a long time. Then his eyes were inexplicably drawn to the reflection of the moon on the Toms River. Paulsen gazed into the blue-white coloring of the moon on the water as the waves moved slowly in and out of the light. Suddenly, just as it had done on previous nights the placid water began to darken and turn red. Seemingly without any warning the moon repeated the trick the water had played and slowly began to bleed red. Paulsen's eyes darted back and forth from the water to the moon and back. He couldn't believe it was happening again.

"Jump Scotty." The ethereal voice came to him from nowhere and everywhere all at once. This was the third night the voice came to him in his sleep, it wasn't the only time the voice had injected itself into his life. He had heard it in the firing range when it told him to put the barrel to his chin and also at the waterfront when it told him to jump in and stay under the water.

"Come on Scotty, jump. You can do it."

On the first night that he found himself on the roof of Reingold Hall, when he heard the voice speak to him he ran as quickly as his feet would take him. He shot through the door and down the stairway, slamming into the wall at the landing and then burst through the door into the hallway. When he slid to a stop in front of the door to room 509 he stopped himself. Scott stood absolutely silent with his eyes pressed shut. When he opened them he stared at the door for another long moment hoping no one had heard him making all that noise. He slowly turned his head from side to side listening for any sounds. He didn't hear a thing, but as he reached to push the door open something shot down the hall out of the corner of his eye. It startled him so much that he was frozen. Scott couldn't move. He swallowed hard and turned his head to the left where he saw the movement, but there was nothing there. With a quick push the door opened and being very careful not to wake his roommates he slipped into the room and into his bunk. Lying in his bunk he turned his face into his pillow and realized that he was soaked with sweat.

Last night, the second night that he found himself on the roof of the old building the voice called to him again after a few minutes of staring over the edge. This time he wasn't as startled and turned quickly – hoping to find the culprit who had been harassing him over the past month... but there was no one there. He walked slowly towards the large ventilation duct that sat in the middle of the roof. Scott walked all the way around it but still could not find anyone. Finally he had walked to each corner of the roof and looked down but did not see anyone before returning to his bunk.

But tonight was different.

"Do it."

The moon was full and the entire landscape around him was awash in red. That had not happened before. He could feel the beads of sweat trickling down his forehead and stopping at his eyebrows for just a moment in spite of the cool October air blowing up from the ground.

"You want to jump."

The voice was being more persistent tonight. It had not spoken to him repeatedly before. Yes, tonight was different because Scott knew what the voice wanted him to do and he knew why. He had found the picture left under his pillow. He saw the words written on the back in nearly formed block letters. He had looked in the 1945 yearbook and seen the dedication. He understood when his dream last night had shown him. Then the voices came to him as if they were all around him.

Here beneath the towering pines, by the river blue
Farragut will ever stand, alma mater true

Scott began to mouth the words along with the choir of voices. He was mesmerized until the voice came back to him and jolted him back to the ledge.

"You must!" the voice hissed in his ear.

And now that he understood the entire story, it came together all at once. Scott Paulsen knew that he could indeed help the voice. He could stop it's suffering and torment for these past forty years. He also knew that was not the first one to have been chosen by the voice to help. If he was right, he knew that he would be the last one to have to do it.

Tomorrow was October 31st and the morning reveille would be met with a big Halloween surprise.

Scott Paulsen thought he knew how to put an end to all the madness. He thought he had to jump and that would end the vicious cycle. But there was only one way to find out.

So he jumped.

About the Author

Bruce lives in Suburban Philadelphia with his wife and four children. In addition to writing, he enjoys baseball, playing guitar, reading, church, cooking and being a dad.

Bruce grew up at the Jersey Shore and graduated from Admiral Farragut Academy in Pine Beach, NJ where he first fell in love with reading and writing under the guidance of Jeff Cain and Verne Romefelt. From those early influences Bruce was introduced to and fell in love with Shakespeare, Marlow, Henry James and Nathaniel Hawthorne.

Bruce's other works including *Sands of Time* are available at all major outlets in both print and eBook formats (Kindle, iBookstore and Smashwords).

Bruce can be reached on his website, http://www.bruceasarte.com on Facebook or GoodReads. Be sure to follow @bsarte on Twitter.

For the best stories from the best authors come by and visit Bucks County Publishing on the web!